CW00326507

MITCH ROBERTS,

I hobbled to the kit[...] mud coffee. I made some oatmeal and drank orange juice. I set the alarm for six o'clock and took a nap. When I woke lightning creased the sky and there was sudden thunder. The sky shimmered from ghostly orange light. My head was dull as a cinder block but the double vision cleared.

I washed my face and stared at the scarecrow in the mirror. He looked something like me, except that he had bandages on his head and his eyes were ringed by blue-black bruises. He was smiley and a helpful sort of guy, but he had a mean streak and no ambition. I brushed his teeth and told him to be polite and not drink so much.

"Mitch Roberts is one of the more likeable heroes who have taken up the gun and the plastic badge in recent years."

Loren Estleman

SNAKE EYES

Gaylord Dold

IVY BOOKS • NEW YORK

IVY BOOKS
Published by Ballantine Books

Library of Congress Catalog Card Number: 87-90849

ISNB - 0-8041-0146-9

Manufactured in the United States of America

First Edition: September 1987

To Christy Anne with love

ONE

The first Saturday of May mamboed into my musty office and sashayed around the place, curvy and luscious as Rita Hayworth in a terry robe. I put some coffee on the hotplate to perk, then reclined in my captain's chair to let Rita walk her milky hands through my hair. I'd been away from the office for more than a week, and it felt wonderful to close my eyes as the scent of lilac, sunshine, and fresh coffee shoved aside the winter smell of disuse. Outside, robins rhapsodized, a few Fords and Chevys tooted and chugged, and Rita slid a hand around my wallet. When I opened my eyes, I stared at a stack of bills and collection notices piled neatly on my desk. The bills and collection notices stared back. I poured myself a hot cup of coffee and started feeling not-so-wonderful.

I sat back in the blackoak chair and slid a fingernail under the flap of the gaudiest notice. Inside the envelope cringed a flimsy slip of onionskin bordered in black, accoutered with nice, red letters, demure as a dame along the Pigalle. FINAL NOTICE, it screamed. I folded the slip and shoved it back into its cheap envelope with the window on the side. I closed one eye and shuffled the deck of notices and peeked at the top letter. The top letter was another cheap envelope with a window. I riffled the deck and cut to another cheap envelope with a window. When you're thirty-seven years old and live all alone, you begin to think of two-stepping with collection notices as a segue to Social Security. I hurled the stack of notices to the back edge of my desk and unfurled the sports page. The Bums and the Yanks made me forget about Social Security.

Just then a voice boomed, "It's a matter of life or death." I looked through the wavering coffee steam and followed the sound of the voice to a velvety shadow hidden behind the gauze of the screen door. The velvety shadow merged finally into the oafish head and neck of Jake the barber. Jake owned a two-chair shop next door to my office.

"Well, come on in," I said. I hadn't seen Jake in a month, just the amount of time it had taken to grease the wheels of my latest squeaky murder case and unravel the bonds of a mucky trial at the county courthouse. The murder solved itself, as murders will, but the murder trial itself had evolved into a nasty evil cavern. In the end, a crusty, alcoholic D.A. had stumbled out of the cavern with a conviction in the buttonhole of his gabardine suit, saving my own noodle from the soup. It had meant weeks on the witness stand, a gun under the pillow at night. In the end, a bad guy went to prison for thirty years. By the time he got out we'd both be too old to make a fuss. In the meantime my pal Andy Lanham in Homicide still circled the house late at night, and I hadn't seen Jake.

Jake tossed aside the screen and staggered in, trailing a wake of cigar smoke. He wore a white barber's smock above plaid pants and white orthopedic shoes. The shoes were broken at the heels. His red face glistened with sweat and turmoil. "I'm foiled," he said sadly. "I'm flat foiled."

"Someone run off with your Nat Cole collection?" I asked.

"Worse."

"Leper take a bath with your wife?"

"Worse. Much, much worse." Jake rubbed a meaty

hand across his face, unlocked his knees, and fell straight down into a leather chair tipped against the wall. He focused his eyes and unholstered a pint of Overholt rye from his hip.

Jake and I went way, way back. We'd met five years before, when I was moving into my offices, deerstalker, magnifying glass, and all. We both toured the economic countryside sniping for rent payments, and we shared an interest in whiskey and baseball. Once in a while, we snuck out to fish for cats in a farm pond north of town. We were suitably philosophical and good-natured about misfortune. Each of us had killed Germans in the war and now dreamed about it at night. We talked a lot about baseball. We never talked about the war.

Jake proffered a glug of rye. I refused.

"You been sober lately, I hear," he said.

"Couple or three weeks. The trial."

"I hear there was some news about a gal with black hair, figure cute as a goldfish."

"News travels fast in a town like this," I said. I pushed a cigarette into my mouth and stoked. Jake smashed into the rye and grimaced as he swallowed, then ran a white arm of smock across his lips. There had been a black-haired gal, but there wasn't anymore.

"What the hell is that like? Being sober, I mean," he asked.

"Rough." I laughed. "Rough as hell. I see things clearly. Fuzz on a woman's leg, warts, harelips. I wake up before eleven. I talk to the mailman, change the oil in the car. Senses too sharp." I wanted to let the melodrama unfold in its own time, with its own internal force, the way the villain ties the heroine to the railroad tracks, the way the story unfolds every time. I smoked. Jake gulped the rye. In the rectangle of sky outside the screen door, a cobalt patch floated, one white cloud suspended in the patch. A green frieze of elm slanted into the cobalt patch. The green frieze danced in the breeze. Two cardinals played on silvered limbs of the elms, each bird chipping a staccato song into the wind. Time washed up on the sand.

Finally I said, "Okay, Jake, spill it. What's so bad it has you by the Overholt on a beautiful Saturday morning?"

"My boys are going to college," he said.

I nodded sympathetically. Jake relaxed. He possessed two sons, each a lopsided version of a rural lumberyard. They wrestled at East High, and I knew Jake wanted them to join the army like their old man had.

From his slouch, Jake dragged the Overholt to his mouth and sucked. "You been gone," he said. "I found out a week ago about this college thing. I know I gotta have some extra money. See, I can't send two dopes to college on what a barber makes in a two-hole crapper. No sir."

I smoked. Jake sat back to tell his tale. "Anyway, I find this ad in the newspaper. The state wants a barber to cut the hair of crazy people up in the state hospital. I figure this is going to be a way to make some easy money every Friday night. I check around, see. I gotta bid for the contract, so I get ahold of some guys I know down at the Moose Lodge and they tell me I can probably get the contract for forty cents a head. They got about two hundred crazies up there that need whacking every Friday. That ain't bad money for putting clippers to a wacko's head, right? I figure it'll take me about two minutes each. I'm up there a few hours and back home with the wife, no problem. So, I get the contract."

Jake shook free of the chair and stood in spiraling shafts of sunlight, touching a match to his wet, dead cigar, then chugging a dense smoke ring into Rita's lovely visage. Outside, a robin coughed. I listened and smoked.

"Anyway, I drive to the hospital last night after I close the shop. A matron who looks like Bela Lugosi meets me and takes me into the basement of a redbrick bunker and there they are, two hundred crazies lined up like ducks. Bellowing and slobbering like ducks, too, they were.''

''It's only a haircut, right?'' I said. My encouragement stumbled and fell into the gutter.

''Yeah,'' said Jake. ''We got pinheads, cretins, freaks, dwarfs. Old ladies acting like flies without wings. The matron sets me up with a cane chair and a bottle of alcohol. What's the alcohol for, I ask. The matron grins and buzzes away. I start shaving. The third pinhead down the line, I shave through a wart and the blood starts to fly. Dwarfs and pinheads and cretins screaming bloody murder. The old dames spin like dervishes and shout. Me, I grab the alcohol and splash it on the wart on the pinhead. Rest of the night I'm burring heads and throwing alcohol. Took me twelve hours to earn eighty bucks. Knock off ten bucks for gas, ten bucks for whiskey, ten bucks for two pairs of scissors someone stole, and two hours lost at the shop. Some deal.''

''How long does the contract last?'' I asked.

Jake shoved the Overholt into the hip of his smock. He tossed me a wan smile. ''Two years,'' he said. ''Two long years.''

''What happens if you don't show?''

''Not show up for the state contract?'' Jake shook his head knowingly. ''State license board sneezes on me and I'm covered with snot.''

In the parking lot outside a muffled rumble pushed itself through the breeze. What seemed to be a cream and beige Packard crunched the gravel and stopped. A shawl of dust drifted into the sun. Somewhere, a sweet motor churned like the Gulf Stream off Cornwall.

''I gotta get back to the shop,'' Jake said. He stood with his back to me.

''You know, Mitch. The last guy had the state haircut contract was named Snively. I knew him. Had a shop down on Broadway. Couldn't ever figure what happened to the guy. I hadn't seen him at the lodge in a year.'' Jake went to the screen door and stood, exhaling smoke into the clear, blue atmosphere. He puffed dramatically, then leaned his head against the mesh. ''That guy Snively. I saw him last night. I swear he was in line waiting for a shave.'' Jake went out. He pushed his head against the screen again, his face a Halloween mush of disillusionment.

''You believe this shit?'' He laughed.

I settled back, thinking again about collection notices and black-haired women. A melodic creak of elm came in the spring breeze, then I heard, unmistakably, two thumps of very solid steel. Another velvety shadow appeared at the screen. This time the shadow was dark and narrow. Sunlight streamed around the shadow, lending form to the gestalt of an exclamation mark on a field of daisies. The door opened.

''Yes?'' I said. It was a formal yes, out of place as a showgirl at the senior prom.

''Mr. Roberts?''

''You got it, pal. Come on in.''

The exclamation point entered, wary and alert. The guy wasn't quite tall enough for oxygen at sea level, but he was tall. Everything about his form was trim and well-done, but there was nothing skinny about it. He wore a dark blue windbreaker and wool slacks. The slacks were expensive and held a crease that would have sliced sirloin. Half moons of sunlight danced diamond shapes on alligator shoes. The guy stared at a spot on the wall behind my left shoulder. I shrugged, trying to shake the stare away from the wall. The stare stayed put.

''You sure you got the right place?'' My office was no place for wool slacks and alligator shoes. If the guy belonged to the Packard, then he didn't know that Packards didn't slum.

''You're Mitch Roberts, aren't you?''

''Yeah.''

"Then I've got the right place." The guy stood. I sat. Then I saw the dog, motionless as malice aforethought. The dog didn't say anything, he just sat. One of the guy's thin hands held a leather circle. At the end of the circle a spike collar wound around the dog's neck. The dog was pure Doberman, brainy, sleek, and inscrutable. A brown wedge of fur melted from his chest into a sea of silky black, shiny as his master's alligator shoes. Two frozen eyes drilled from the dog's head into my throat. It was a short ride in the country, imagining several hundred sharp teeth tearing chunks of detective.

"You've got me at a disadvantage," I said. The guy gazed illogically. The dog did not.

"I'm Jules Reynard," he said.

His voice was all alto, calm and solid. Reynard stood unwavering as a taproot. He had square shoulders, a line of jaw shaped like a horseshoe. Beneath olive skin you could imagine fine, white bone. His hair was an ebony shell, gray at the ear. For the life of me the guy looked like Gary Cooper.

"Have a seat, Mr. Reynard."

He did, shuffling slowly with purpose. Reynard swished the leash. The dog moved with him like a disembodied shade. My throat began to sweat. From the barbershop erupted morning radio. Reynard sat and the dog descended to his haunches, two ears like radar spikes.

"What can I do for you, Mr. Reynard?"

"Have you made your decision?"

Reynard reached into the windbreaker and extracted a flashy gold case. He opened the case and took out a cigar the size of a poison dart. He lit the cigar, waiting for a reply. A reply didn't present itself.

"I trust your answer is yes, Mr. Roberts. I don't detect any reluctance in your demeanor."

"Forgive me, Mr. Reynard. My demeanor is confused

right now. Suppose you circle the bases, wave to the crowd, and step back to the plate.''

Reynard inhaled smoke with deliberation. A faint five o'clock shadow dusted his jaw. I supposed it was a permanent fixture. ''I don't believe I understand,'' he said. His stare grew its own whiskers.

''Look, Mr. Reynard. I really don't know who you are, what you want, or where we go from here. Maybe we'd better get in step before we scuff up our new shoes.'' Next door, I heard Jake singing to a Nat Cole number.

''You didn't get my letter, then?'' Reynard asked.

I leaned over the desk and shuffled the collection notices again. A second shuffle produced a rag-weave envelope without a window. Serious swirls of black ink had melted into the rag weave, letters the size and shape of King John's signature on the Magna Carta.

I put the letter down carefully. The return address read *Black Fox Ranch. Augusta, Kansas.* ''What does it say?'' I asked.

Reynard relaxed. The dog stayed put. ''The letter tells you I'll be by on Saturday. It says something important is bothering me and that I want to discuss retaining your confidential services. It asks you to call me if the time is inconvenient.'' Reynard stabbed an ironic period to the words.

''Why me?'' I asked.

''I've been in the hospital during the past weeks. There has been little to do save play chess and think. I recall an article in the local newspaper that mentioned your name as a detective and a witness in a local murder case. There was mention of your competence, but little else. It seemed enough to go on for the meantime.'' A faint smile snared the edge of Reynard's mouth and tugged. ''Perhaps there is more than one Mitch Roberts in Wichita. Perhaps you don't read your mail.''

''I've taken some time off,'' I said.

"I don't blame you. A six-week murder trial is withering fire. I must say, it looks as if you hold up well."

"I've been in withering fire plenty. I never hold up, particularly not well. I was lucky."

"Nevertheless," Reynard said.

"Nevertheless," I said back. Reynard sat, thinking. Uncertainty blundered around the room.

"Mr. Roberts," Reynard said at last. "I've lived a long time not needing a private detective. Most people do. Under those conditions of life, there are no criteria for choosing one when it comes up. I saw your name, and it stuck. Do you have any objections?"

"I'm sorry, Mr. Reynard. I don't object if you read every newspaper in Duluth. It's just that right now I can't take on any cases. I'm worn down and tired and behind in every category from repossessing a Dodge to serving an eviction notice. I haven't washed my dishes in six weeks and the moths have subdivided my wardrobe. Whatever problems you have, Mr. Reynard, you'll have to take them down the block. I can recommend some good people."

I felt bad saying the words. I'd stared into the gullet of a fat lawyer. The gullet called me liar and two-bit. At the end of the trial a black-haired woman had folded the deal and sold her seat. Any day I expected Satan to follow suit. It was no excuse to snap at Reynard.

"Look, Mr. Reynard," I said. "You may have a problem I could help with, I don't know. I know I've got half a dozen steady clients. These guys keep me in white bread and cheap beer. I serve their papers, repossess their cars, find their wives. They send me a check, small and comforting. If I didn't have those clients, I wouldn't make enough money to spit at a crippled newsie."

Reynard jerked the leash. The dog went on to its belly. For a while we sat surrounded by sunlight, hearing the cardinals and the Chevys, Jake caterwauling in his barbershop. Reynard seemed to look at the floor.

"Please hear me out," he said. The quiet drowned his voice.

"You want some coffee?" I said. Reynard nodded slowly. I handed him a cup and he handled it unsteadily. "All right, Mr. Reynard. Shoot."

He sipped the coffee. "Have you ever had your life come apart?" he asked.

"But yes," I said. "Three or four times if you don't count finding out I couldn't hit a curveball."

"I'm fifty-four years old. I've just spent two weeks in the hospital. I've been ill for six months. I may regain my strength, but the doctors say it will take some time. Maybe never, they say." Reynard waited for me to speak. It didn't seem necessary. "You see, I've controlled my own life, achieved a measure of success, made some money. But in the last year I've lost some bets. I don't mind losing on a square table and right dice."

"One dot short on the dice these days?"

"One short, one too many. What is the difference?"

I lit a Lucky. "Go on," I said.

"One of my businesses is out of hand. I want you to find out why."

"I know a good accountant," I said. "I imagine you do, too."

"It's gone beyond that point," Reynard said. He rested his hand on the dog's ear. A fly buzzed around the dog's snout, but there was no flinch. "There's more."

"Deal it up," I said.

"The illness was arsenic."

"Someone tried to kill you?"

"Possible. Probable, moving to likely. Arsenic is hard to pick up from a dish of strawberries."

"I understand the best recipes leave it out."

Ash drifted from Reynard's cigar. A wad of it dropped to the floor. It was a curious display for a guy in creased wool pants and alligator shoes. Reynard puffed gently, savoring the smoke. I sat thinking, not savoring a thing.

Finally, Reynard said, "There've been some personal problems. Problems of the kind one doesn't admit. Contorted things. You remember, Mr. Roberts, I asked you if your life had ever come apart?"

"I remember."

"I need some patchwork on my life."

I sighed. The sigh hit bottom. I poured some coffee and motioned to Reynard for a refill. Nothing budged, not even the drizzly stare he had affixed to the wall. A vague weariness wiggled to the surface of the past six weeks and poked its head above the slime. In six weeks I'd spent sixteen dollars on bad courthouse coffee and earned half that in fees. At this point, life's problems were bad breath on a first date and the only mouthwash was real money.

"Let's see," I said. "Skip tracing is twenty-five a day. Repossession without a gun, twenty-five a day. Service of process, ten bucks a pop, plus gas. Let's just say I haven't put a price on human patchwork."

"Ten thousand dollars," said Reynard. "Ten thousand now, a bonus of ten thousand when you're done. I cover all expenses, no questions asked. I've got the money."

I relaxed into a surprised clump. Rita swished my way and rubbed the fuzzy, cashmere curves of her sweater against my forehead. Her breasts thumped inside the fuzz. She roped her long red hair around my neck, giving me a good, long whiff of perfume. Four shiny nails scratched my chin, then lifted it toward two lips the color of sweetheart roses. We kissed. Rita struggled with the wallet. I devoured her next twenty thousand kisses. Reynard stood and switched the dog's leash. The dog rose.

"What's a life worth, anyway?" I said.

"Precisely," said Reynard. "Perhaps you can work mine into your fee schedule."

"I see your point." A man could fit plenty of white bread and bad beer into twenty thousand dollars.

Reynard walked slowly to the screen door. "I'd like you to come out to the ranch tonight. Black Fox Ranch—east of Rose Hill, south of Augusta. It's easy to find, check a county map. About eight o'clock?"

"I'm not making any promises."

"Fine," Reynard said. "We'll have dinner, play a game of chess, perhaps." Reynard pushed clumsily through the door. There was a solid, steel thud, then the sound of the Packard toiling in gravel.

Saturday devolved into repossessions. I paid some bills. Later, I drove through deserted streets to my rooms in an old Victorian on Sycamore. I waltzed with the dirty dishes and took a nap. In one dream, Rita cooed a siren song, washed whirling to a rocky deep.

TWO

Magenta sun swept my three rooms, shafts and streaks breaking through stained glass, glass shimmering like bloodstone. I lay on an old brass bed looking past the V-shape of my feet at the rough, triangular head of Francis the cat, who sat preening himself for an evening on the town. Francis stroked his tongue along a gray flank, then pecked at a hairy slab of right ear. Beyond my feet, beyond the gray head of Francis, wind and sun played tag in an elm current. Limbs bumped rhythmically like a steady, green symphony. The dust in the air vibrated. Except for the sound of children far away, the silence itself seemed deep as the green symphony outside. Francis rolled onto his back, stretched his stomach, and yawned.

I pushed a pillow against the bedstead and sat upright. My rooms wound through the bottom of an old Victorian on Sycamore Street, across from a minor league ballpark. I'd lived here since coming home from the war. The unconcern of a Kansas City slumlord made it appear as if I could live here until Yorick himself won the Irish Sweepstakes. Or at least until the Athletics won the pennant. My kitchen was full of muscatel empties; the main sitting room and bedroom was divided from the kitchen by an oak bookcase and stained glass window. The room itself was airy, full of the disheveled remnants of chess games, ball scores, and fishing tackle. Late at night I enconced myself in a gray overstuffed chair haloed in the aromatic gleam of a brass lamp, smoking Latakia in a calabash, playing the games of Alekhine or Capablanca. The large room let into an alcove, with an antique oak table and my unique collection of dead cacti. Bay windows encircled the alcove. It was through the bay windows that the green symphony leaked.

Time, dense as regret, passed through these rooms. I dozed and dreamed, trying to suffocate the memory of the murder trial and the black-haired woman. Nothing seemed to work.

After a while, I rose and poured a glass of muscatel from the last gallon in the refrigerator. I stared through the back screen, watching the wind in the weedy backyard, the chickens and the rabbits in the hutches, looking down the tangled alley that disappeared down a row of Victorians like mine. A rickety staircase ascended from my porch to the rooms of Mrs. Thompson, an old lady who lived upstairs.

I finished the muscatel. While I showered, the memory of the black-haired woman revealed a soft line of throat, mahogany hair lying against a white sheet, fibrous as an exotic plant at the bottom of the sea. The steam cleared. I shaved and washed behind my ears, then took a look inside the bathroom closet. There were a few pairs of cords, some shiny dress pants, half a dozen wool shirts, Red Wing boots, hiking vests, and a few tweed coats. Little enough. I put on a clean flannel shirt, a pair of brown cords, and a tweed coat. There wasn't much choice. I brushed my teeth and combed the ash-blond mop that passed for hair.

I was ready for dinner with Jules Reynard. Save for the lack of a tulip in my lapel, I thought I deserved a C+ at least. I went through the back door, leaving the ghostly woman with the black hair and the murder trial behind.

I went down the steps to the rabbit hutch. Mrs. Thompson huddled by it, covered by her gray housecoat, her white hair rippled by wind as if an electric current had passed through it. She was short, hunched, and her movements were sparrowlike, stuttered, and cluttered by indecision.

"Mr. Mitch," she screamed. "Oh, Mr. Mitch!" Mrs. Thompson was nearly deaf. "They've got two new babies!"

Two small rabbits slept in the hutch, patched white and black both. I held Mrs. Thompson by the shoulders, then put my mouth to her ear.

"What are their names?" I yelled.

Mrs. Thompson recoiled. She stood, seeming almost to fall. Finally she said, "Faith and Hope."

I winked, got into the Fairlane, and started the engine. I waved to the old lady. She poked slices of carrot at the noses of the sleeping babies.

I rumbled through alley chuckholes and drove east on Maple Street, away from the setting sun. The Black Fox covered six hundred acres on the near edge of the Flint Hills, twenty miles southeast of Wichita. I fished the creeks and farm ponds in that country, and knew a country lane that I used as a shortcut. The lane wound through dense hedges along a river bottom. Five miles from town I rolled into farmland crowded by oak and elm scrub. The road descended through a series of creek bridges, iron monuments built by the CCC during the Depression. The thicket thickened gradually, until the spark of spring stars dwindled to scattered streaks obscured by shade. Frogs and crickets clattered. Puffy clouds darkened. In the deep, the lane bordered a meandering river surrounded by sycamore and oak. In that place there was no light or sound, save for the frogs and the crunch of tires on gravel. I flicked on the radio, filling the Fairlane with yellow glow and Artie Shaw. Washington Irving disappeared into the fog. Then the road ascended, turned south, and at the same time became a black macadam strip.

The strip sped past widening swales of green winter wheat. The wheat drifted in the wind. I let cigarette smoke into the evening, thinking about Jules Reynard and the curious problems he had announced. He spoke of his own murder in the calmest terms, approaching it like a chessboard. I had felt uncomfortable in his presence. The sound of his money had made me feel worse. It was the sound of money seeping into the crevices of a man's soul, corroding it like poison. In the detective business, there is money that obliges a good job and money that obliges a good cry. But Reynard's money obliged too much.

Wheat fields evolved into pasture. Pasture rolled and fell, and in the declivities cattle grazed. Spring stars—Regulus, Leo, Spica, and Pollux—popped into focus, becoming points on a field of cobalt and mauve. Lights flickered in the distance at the Black Fox. I swung the car into a cute lane and drove along more pasture. A three-strand white fence separated the lane from manicured farm buildings. Quarter horses munched prairie grass. The lane wove around a horseshoe lake that wrapped around a large house. The house was L-shaped, brick and wood. I parked in a copse of Scotch pine and jumped out of the car. I lit a Lucky. The front door was big and heavy. There was a knocker, and I knocked.

A cowboy opened the door. He was average size, with striking, angular features. His arms and hands were big. He wore a blue work shirt, chinos, cowboy boots, and a dark blue vest. He stood there in the Scotch pine shadow.

"I'm Mitch Roberts," I said. "Here to see Mr. Reynard."

"Right," he said. "Come on in." The cowboy flicked

a hand at a Doberman. Wind creased the cowboy's blond hair.

I went into a room the size of Cleveland. One whole wall was glass. Past the glass was the horseshoe lake. The lake glowed, lamplight dancing on the surface. Behind the lake, pasture waded uphill into a purple sunset. A Hogan three-iron away from me, carpeted stairs descended to a sunken area. In the sunken area were two zebra couches and a few stiff chairs, a mahogany table, decanters, and a chess set in onyx. On one wall was a well-stocked bar, the bar snaking along to what looked like a conservatory. The conservatory was dark, but the darkness emitted a smell of damp palm. Silver-barreled lamps cast a dim glow. In one cool circle of lamplight sat a black Doberman, head on paws, eyes alert and focused. Except for the Doberman, the place looked like Rick's Café American.

I followed the cowboy and the Doberman to a glass door. The cowboy opened the glass, and I went out onto a flagstone patio littered by iron tables, lounges, and deck chairs. The patio followed the lake's contour, five feet above the surface.

The cowboy said, "You'll find Mr. Reynard at the end. Follow the blue lights." The cowboy went inside. I walked to the edge of the patio, followed the blue deck lights, and stood at the last iron table. Reynard sat, hands placed calmly. He wore a black turtleneck and the same wool slacks. A mild breeze ruffled his black hair. In the evening light, he made an articulate form. The smoke from his black cigar leaked into the wind.

"Good evening, Mr. Roberts," he said.

I sat down. "How long have you been blind?" I asked.

Reynard's free hand fell to the flank of the Doberman. The Doberman crouched, the leash tangled at his neck.

"I wondered how long you'd take," Reynard said. "Tell me about the evening. What does it look like?"

"It's lovely," I said. A whippoorwill sang.

"No," Reynard said. "What do you see?"

"The wheat is liquid jade. The lake is black, wheat reflections and the wheat itself rising up from the pasture into a sunset gone gold and mauve. Then a line of elm in the west, a few stars twinking."

I smoked. Reynard was quiet.

"You're good. Why the game?" I asked.

"I pretend," Reynard said. "When others know, it twists things out of shape. When did you figure it out?"

"Two doors slammed when you drove up to my office. I thought it odd that only one person came in. Your stare just missed my face. It got to me after a while. You let cigar ash drop."

Reynard smiled as if the smile escaped from somewhere deep. He faced the receding sun, one purple gash illuminating the square set of his face. I gathered the empty liquidity of his sight. There was no injury or disease in the eyes, just cold pales of brown. Each movement for him was a measured volume of uncertainty and dread. He poured the volume into a beaker of his own needs. Whippoorwills hid in the prairie grass, singing sadly.

Reynard spoke. "I concentrate on your voice. I direct my own movement to the sound. It's not perfect, of course. You detected it quite quickly."

"It wasn't that easy. How did you do the chair?"

"My secret."

"Anyway, Mr. Reynard, it wasn't that easy. The gaze and the dog and the car doors made me wonder. Nothing special. I offered you a cup of coffee and you didn't move a muscle."

"Oh," Reynard said. "Something small always spoils the game. I can't tell if you don't apologize and fumble. Most people do. Why not you?"

"No reason."

The cowboy moved behind us. He set down two glasses of beer. He went away.

"I trust you're a beer drinker," Reynard said.

"Cheap beer and white bread," I answered. Reynard held his glass. I clinked it, and we drank.

"I've been blind for a few years. At first shapes and now just shapes of shapes. Diabetes. It's been part of my problem lately."

I pulled at the beer. Going down, it was like silk along a woman's leg, slick and shiny. Jeweled rays played in the glass, reflecting an evening sky itself silken; lapis lazuli edged by black elms; mauve rays snaking along a ragged lee of horizon; fireflies blinking above the lake. A single damask swath hovered above the treeline. The barrel lamps inside the house threw a burning shaft into the fluid night.

"You remember being sighted?" I asked.

"No," he said. That was it. A "No" welled up from the pit, a maelstrom of an answer. Reynard drank his beer.

"Well, you do fine. You had me fooled."

"Tiresias keeps me headed in the right direction." Reynard patted the dog's head. "I've blind eyes. He, a blind soul, blind to the world. He leads, I follow. Blind and sighted leading the sighted and blind. That's my secret of the chair."

Reynard ran a hand through the dog's ears. The dog flicked his head, ears perked.

"You saw Creon inside," Reynard said. "They're killers."

"They roam the place?"

"At night," answered Reynard. He restarted his cigar. I smoked a cigarette.

"I hope you're hungry," Reynard said. "I'm serving a small fillet, mushrooms, green salad. I'm afraid it's nothing fancy. I've got some good whiskey." I nodded, thinking how stupid that was.

The cowboy served with a tray. There was a bottle of whiskey and a pitcher of ice water on it. Blue lamps rimmed the patio, each dipping a reflection into the water. I ate the steak quickly, a good fillet done medium-rare. I poured two whiskeys, and we drank together.

"I've made a lot of money in my time, Mr. Roberts," Reynard said. "I made most of it before I became blind. I don't want to lose it now. That's why you're here. You won't be underpaid, but it could be dangerous."

Reynard sipped his whiskey. Now his voice was a lower register, more a growl, miles of trudging in mud behind it. The change startled me.

"Suppose you tell me how it is."

"I don't let jakelegs fuck with me," he said. "I don't like it. We are supposed to be businessmen, not thugs." Reynard stopped his voice at a dull roar. He seemed embarrassed at his anger. He fell back in his chair, forming his fingers into a steeple, very businesslike. He went on. "I'm a businessman. I raise cattle here, good quarter horses. I've got some oil on the other side of the section. There's no problem with the money right now. Under these conditions, it makes itself."

"I've never had that happen," I said. It was true. For me love and money were the same. Difficult to get and hold on to.

"It hasn't always been that way," Reynard said in reply. "Suppose we take a walk. We'll talk. I'll show you the place. Pour me a whiskey, will you?" I poured.

Reynard held the leash in his left hand, carried the whiskey in his right. Tiresias led the way along the patio, above the water, then down a slope past the edge of the ranch. We slowly descended a hillock, stone steps cut into the hill, stone walls on either side of the steps. At the bottom was a corral. A few horses grazed at troughs.

"Good-looking, don't you think?"

"Very," I said, leaning an arm on the fence. I hopped the fence and the horses grew alert.

"Get back here," Reynard said. I hopped the fence again. "These quarters aren't broke. None of them are. They'll knock you down as soon as spit." Each horse was sleek and strong-looking.

"When I was in the hospital two of my horses died. Throats torn, slashed." Tiresias led us around the rim of the corral. An open-faced shed held tack and hay.

"I ate a bowl of berries three weeks ago and damn near died. That's when they hit the horses."

"Day or night?" I asked.

"Had to be night. Colby would have been here otherwise."

"Colby?"

"The man who let you in."

"Colby handle the dogs?" I asked.

"Same as me," Reynard answered. He shook the leash, and we sauntered into open prairie, rolling past farm ponds like shiny nickels in a velvet glove.

"Look, Mr. Reynard. I'm not a bodyguard. With your money you could hire plenty of muscle. For that, I don't have the guts or the stamina. I couldn't sucker-punch Little Bo Peep."

Reynard said nothing; we walked.

I said, "I drink too much. I don't do long-haul observation. I get bored too easy." Behind us, the lights of the ranch dove into tunnels of sunset. The Flint Hills grass rustled like woman's hair on a clean sheet. The house had a thick, shingle roof shadowed by the pines. Otherwise, there were no trees on the prairie, just the line of elm and oak toward town.

I went on. "Look, Mr. Reynard. You don't pop into my office and offer me twenty thousand for police work. You never mentioned the police."

"No police," he said.

I followed Reynard along barbed-wire fence. Black Angus strolled dumbly. Tiresias tugged Reynard along a path worn in the pasture, threading the dark and the prairie. Wind whooshed through the Scotch pines. We were in front of the house. I sensed something else tugging at Reynard, something strong and lethal like pride, the inability to come to terms with the contortions of fate.

"Let's go inside," Reynard said. "Maybe I can get through this with a brandy."

I followed him back into the huge living room, then down the carpeted stairs. The room breathed inaudibly. Tiresias curled up on a white shag rug. Between the zebra couches stood the onyx chess set, and a decanter of brandy. Reynard fumbled for the decanter.

"Help me with this," he said. I poured two brandies. A torque of shadow enveloped the room.

"I'm a gambler," Reynard said. "I make money because there are more ways to make seven than to make six. I started out with the Canyon Club."

Cheap detectives don't go to the Canyon Club. At the Canyon a man was expected to fade ten dollars without breaking a sweat.

"I've heard of it," I said.

"Well, that's me. Part of me, anyway. Enough to make a difference. I buy booze at two bucks, break the bottle into twenty shots, and sell the shots for two bucks each. Overhead is protection and good food. I make a tidy profit. I've got a wire service on Douglas Street above a bowling alley. We pay for a few good dance bands." Reynard took out a cigar. I lit it for him.

"Somebody is skimming," he said.

"You want me to find out."

"I want you to find out."

"Suppose it's just bad business."

"You bet," he said. "And my horses are committing suicide."

"I see what you mean."

"Look, Mr. Roberts. The liquor and dice business isn't crowded anymore. We've got some small fry around town running games in the back room. But after the war, the boys in Kansas City consolidated. For the last ten years the name of the game has been business, not muscle. Just a dance band, some green felt, and a few bucks to the widows and orphans. You get it?"

"In spades," I replied.

"Since I've been sick, it's been tough keeping track. I can't involve the boys in Kansas City and I can't involve the police."

"What's your hunch?"

"Gus Canard manages the Canyon. He bags the money, makes a set of books at the club. Colby picks the books up and we go over them every week. We make a second set for the government, then bank the money. A skim could take place anywhere down the line."

"Colby?"

"I don't see how. He's been with me since the war."

"Canard?"

"Anywhere. Gus could be on the take. One of the dealers. Hell, it could be the damn busboy."

"You talk this over with Canard?"

"No."

"How do you propose I get close to the operation?" I hoped this question would end the game. The Canyon was downtown in an uptown world, white napkins and a gold ring. I smoked for a while, watching the night brew a concoction. Tiresias slept, one flank harrumphed by doggie dreams.

"Stickman job open at the club. You're a natural," Reynard said.

"But that puts me out of circulation. Those steady clients, you remember?"

"How much circulation can you get from twenty thousand?"

I lit a wooden match. Sulfur flared.

"You said you had some personal problems, Mr. Reynard. Skimming isn't personal." I touched the match to another cigarette. Reynard sat inside a block of steely emptiness. He blew smoke into the lamplight.

"I've married a young woman. I did it at the time my sight was going, perhaps out of fear of the dark. There are worse things. This is one of them."

I didn't speak.

"Her name is Agnes. She spends her time in town, at the Canyon. Making a fool of both of us. She comes and she goes and she changes clothes. She acts stupid and gay. I want her stopped."

"It's hardly my line, Mr. Reynard. Grown-up people have a way of going off."

"You know what I mean," he snapped. I poured two more brandies. Reynard gathered himself and maneuvered to the chess set. He moved a white king pawn two squares. "Tell me your move when you make it. At times, I'll ask you to describe the position. I may ask a question."

In five moves the game became a King's Gambit. I offered a pawn, mucking the position.

"I told you," Reynard said. "I want my life repaired. It's worth money to me. You tell me about Agnes, and I'll do the rest."

I stood. "We'll finish the game later, Mr. Reynard. For now, it sounds all right to me. Let me sleep on it?"

"Of course," Reynard answered. "But tomorrow."

I went out the big doors into the *whoosh* of pine, the smell of grass and cattle. A wind chime tinkled. Two canoes by a boathouse on the lake clicked sterns. I got into the Fairlane and lit a cigarette and sat smoking. A shadow pressed against the glass in the conservatory. The shadow moved deliberately back into the dark and silence of the palms.

I backed the Fairlane around a purple martin house and into the lane. I drove north on the black macadam to the main highway to town. The shortcut hit bottom alone.

THREE

I drove slowly to the eastern rim of town. A pale moon shed metallic dust on the big houses of the rich, on palaces full of good scotch and hot gossip. Eastborough dozed painlessly in the dim glow; huge lawns rolled away to an organdy maze of maple and pin oak. The sky blinked and grew opaque, roads and streets drew into narrow lanes lined by honeysuckle and spirea; in the soundless evening there came the *plop* of tennis ball and racket, a sound as clear and unmistakable as money changing hands. I never felt cheated driving among the houses of the rich. I always imagined that behind the pearly gleam of wealth there lurked a savage and uncompromising poverty of spirit, a sordid tale or two, the final shaggy skeleton whipping in the closet breeze. I knew it wasn't true, but I never felt cheated thinking it.

At Hillside I cruised along the ups and downs of College Hill, draining myself through the sieve of dwindling traffic, smoking my cigarette, imagining being keelhauled by a wad of dollar bills along an ocean of crap tables. The wind grieved for winter, the shadows ducked along the brick street. Trees swirled. I went south toward the Canyon Club.

Anxiety found a peephole and peeped. I'd done worse than work for bootleggers and gamblers. Kansas had banned the open saloon in 1862. You could get a glass of beer downtown until midnight, you could buy a half-pint of rye in a shack across the tracks, or you could make your own. What you couldn't get was a square drink and a good steak, maybe a dance with a blonde not your mother. There are some people who don't mind drinking weak beer in a cold tavern. And there are some people who don't mind buying rye from an Okie in bib-overalls. But there are a few who would just as soon drink French wine and listen to the accordion with the lamps low. But a nightclub was an open saloon and against the law. As the man says, Kansas staggers to the poll to vote dry.

I'd known for years that small nightclubs flourished in the cracks between law and order. Now I knew that Jules Reynard ran the Canyon with help from Kansas City. I didn't bother to fault him for it. If the people wanted a steak bad enough to corrupt the police, then let them corrupt the police. Money had greased the law since time began and it wasn't up to me to hatchet reality. Time would end before they stopped making dice.

At a roostertail on Hillside I stopped at a shabby hut and bought a pint of vodka. I put the vodka in the glove box, then drove farther into the purlieu of south Wichita. South from College Hill, Wichita levels to a demented straggle of clapboard and tarpaper, traps slapped together willy-nilly during the war, and allowed to wind down like cheap clocks. This part of town was full of Okies, rusted Plymouths, abandoned appliances, dense air smelling of garbage and rendered guts. Between goat bleats, you could hear chickens squawk.

The Canyon Club sat on a small knoll at one dead end of Hillside, overlooking a snipe of brick street. A dirty creek meandered in the thicket behind the knoll and there was the sound of water creeping through brush. A gravel drive circled the knoll. I ascended the gravel and drove into the parking lot. The lot was big and dark, cut into the side of the knoll, which rose above the pavement into a wad of blackjack oak and wild sycamore. Wind rustled in the new green of the oak.

I parked and smoked. Beyond the slender line of broken horizon, a spring storm snapped at the edge of the Flint Hills. Thunder barked far away, and behind the thunder, anarchic flashes bloomed. A seared aroma of ozone emerged. The storm made a molecular progress across the prairie. I thought about hail above the Black Fox Ranch, wind raging through wheat, Reynard blinded to the violent scene. I put the vodka in my back pocket and got out of the car.

The Canyon Club was a block of pink decked out as a Moorish fortress. Behind the block, beneath the shadow of the knoll, the kitchen area was another pink block. Above the kitchen was a limestone office, reached by a stone stair rising from the parking lot to a side door above. The door was dark, stitched with shadows moving with the wind.

Before the war this block of pink had gone by a dozen names. Hades, Flamingo, The Inferno, and The Oasis. Tough guys came and went like Detroit models, worn out before new. In the gloom, I could see enameled scenes of camels, twisted palms, dancing girls. The Canyon was what the boys in Kansas City considered a small club. For Wichita, it was big league all the way. It was decently run and the food was good. There were enough fist fights to make the place entertaining but not too many to scare the girls. There'd been a shooting and a dollop of knifings, but nothing to worry the police. A nice place to go to after church.

I organized for action and walked the gravel path to the kitchen. A shaft of white light pierced the door frame. From inside I heard scrambled voices, the clash of pots and pans. A silly scream escaped. I poked my head around the open jamb to see five or six figures in smocks scurrying about a tomfoolery of aluminum cookery and chopping blocks. I leaned against the door and waited. Beside a row of stoves, a Syrian bent above blue flame, frying enough garlic to choke Mussolini. The Syrian twirled a cleaver with his hefty arm and smacked the blade into the back of a whole chicken. The chicken cracked. Other dark figures in white made salads, washed dishes, bided time, and smoked.

Maye came out of a walk-in freezer. She was small, warped, encased in flour. Her thin body had disappeared nside a cook's apron and gloves. On her feet were black galoshes. With her back toward me she pounded veal. I waited some more. As she turned to wash her mallet, I caught her eye and pushed a finger to my pursed lips. Deliberately, Maye inched to the door with a puzzled look draped on her thin face. Without concern, she leaned against the door, on the other side of the wall from me, hidden for a moment by the wall and the harsh light. I heard her humming softly.

"Mr. Roberts," she sang. A above high C. "What you doing down here with the colored folks?"

"Can I talk to you, Maye?" She turned to the light. "Can you take a break?" I asked.

Maye spread her hands on hips in mock consternation, a wilted look of bewilderment spreading slowly over the sunken features, hollow black eyes, rare cheeks, flat nose. Her eyes glowed with righteous fun. I knew her to be stern as a Mormon tooth fairy, understanding as a whore's midwife.

"You come at the right time," she said. "Dinner is about over. I pound this veal, here. Then I be out."

"Don't say anything, Maye," I said.

"You think I'm a fool?" she said. She grinned all over.

"I'll be under the cutbank."

She turned and crossed to the chopping block. I waited by the Fairlane, hidden in shadow.

I'd been hired by Maye after the war to locate her missing husband. I was a kid, hungry for work, and took the job because I liked Maye and because my phone was silent as a sphinx. For ten years, Maye had saved money, and with her four hundred dollars she wanted me to find Sonny, who'd disappeared behind the Blue Light Lounge in St. Louis, Missouri.

I spent one sultry month in St. Louis, searching union halls, poolrooms, rooming houses, and jails. I bribed a dame in the driver's license bureau, and spent time praying in the Salvation Army by the levee. Time and money ran out. But Maye begged me to keep on and sent me fifty dollars. I gave half of it to a pimp in East St. Louis who knew the dives. I spent a hundred dollars of my own turning over rocks in rescue missions. Finally, I tried the pauper lists of a dozen small towns up and down the Mississippi.

They'd buried Sonny in Belleville, Illinois. Sonny shared ground with dogs, murderers, and orphans. I photographed the grave and ordered a copy of the death certificate. I showed them to Maye and she cried quietly in the small parlor of her shack in the north end. Then she promised me vegetables from her garden: okra, beans, squash, and corn. Now I'd drink whiskey in the evenings and help her work the dirt, digging rows for corn, chopping weeds, swatting flies, hoping for a row of shade against the dreadful yellow sun looping in the west. Maye and I were strangely bonded. She didn't complain about the whiskey. I didn't complain about the snuff she took.

Behind me an arc flashed in the blackjack. Maye appeared, black face smeared with flour and sweat, stripping down her work gloves. She took her time with a cigarette.

"Now what is so important, child?" she said. Maye breathed in the night air. She unwrapped her hair from a cloth and shook herself free from work. "And secret, too. My, my."

I extracted the vodka. Maye swiveled her eyes and drew their dark cavities to the club office. She scuttled back a step and grabbed the vodka. Maye shoved the bottle under her apron and motioned me to follow.

We hiked through a clutch of Packards up a slow rise of knoll, along a path worn into sycamore and hackberry. For a minute we scuttled through thicket buried in shaded undergrowth. Rain smell moved on the wind. A small clearing appeared on a promontory above the pink blocks of the club, and Maye spread herself in the shadow of a blackjack. She opened the vodka, taking an ounce of the shining fluid. It looked like liquid moonglow going down. Below, dance music drifted in darkness. There were the sounds of the kitchen, a rumble of thunder far away. Maye passed me the vodka.

"What *have* you done, Mitch Roberts?" she asked.

I relaxed beneath the oak. The air was lazy and thick with storm. In the parking area, a couple staggered against a black car. Angry voices hammered the night, then the couple entered the car and drove away. I lit a cigarette and turned to the vodka.

"Nice place you got here, Maye," I said.

"I'm in the kitchen ten hours. I come up here to sit and think. Right now I'm so tired they'd have to carry me through the Pearly Gates." Maye took the vodka. Her eyes scanned the outline of the Canyon Club. "You didn't come up here to chat, did you, Mitch Roberts?"

"No, Maye. I didn't."

Maye hit the vodka and passed the bottle. "That's good," she said. "Now, what's wrong?"

"Nothing wrong, Maye. I know you've worked here for quite a while. I want you to answer some questions. It could mean a lot to me. I won't tell anyone."

"All right, Mitch Roberts," Maye said. She settled against the rough bark of the blackjack. "You ask," she said.

"What can you tell me about Jules Reynard?"

"We don't see him anymore, Mitch. He gone blind. Not many know that, but I do."

"What's he like?"

"Very quiet man. He seems to me like a mirror in a dark room. You know there's something in the mirror, but it's just something that moves, that's all." Maye was quiet, thinking. "Then, I've seen him hurt people. He's good to the help, but he doesn't say much."

"You ever see him with his wife?"

"Oh, no," Maye said.

"How about Gus Canard. What's he like?"

Thunder twisted south. The moon dangled in the web of leaf and limb like a sorrowful smile. Maye, covered in white smock and flour, glowed mysteriously. A glint escaped from the bottle as she drank vodka. Someone drove a Buick into the parking lot and stopped. The engine hummed evenly.

"He's no good. His temper is mean and he's got a big smile. I don't know anything worse in a man than that."

"Have you heard anything about skimming at the Canyon?"

"No, sir. Rumors don't get to the kitchen."

I crossed my legs, drinking vodka. The smell of rain advanced, faint and languorous as perfume on a beautiful woman.

"Agnes Reynard," I said. "What about her?"

Maye paused midswig. She wiped her chin, spreading flour and vodka.

"You have a favorite bird?" Maye said with a smile. Somewhere between Maye and me the vodka was at work, throwing hard strikes on the outside corner. We were a ways from the knockdown pitch.

"The crow," I said.

"The crow." Maye laughed. "Hmmph. That's no bird. Your crow, he's like a hobo. Ain't no bird. I mean a songbird, Mitch Roberts."

I thought it over. I was in no hurry. "I'm partial to the morning dove. Lie awake hours listening to him."

"Well," said Maye. "I'm partial to the mockingbird."

"But, Maye," I said. "No mockingbirds in Kansas."

"You don't know, but I was raised in Broken Bow, Oklahoma. Mr. Mockingbird lives in Oklahoma. I'd sit out in the evening with my momma and listen to the song. You see, Mitch, Mr. Mockingbird hasn't got any song of his own. He hears a song and he plays with it. Out comes the prettiest music. He has a hundred songs, all different, all pretty. But he don't have one of his own."

I waited. A peony scent trembled up from the deep. Flower beds surrounded the Canyon Club. Florid shadows escaped from small lamps buried in the peonies, each shade playing on the pink stucco. Couples laughed and argued in the parking lot, then disappeared down the gravel drive and into the gathering maze of mist and traffic-signal flash. I felt vodka torpor draining into the cracks and crevices of my weariness.

"And Agnes?" I asked.

"She's a mockingbird, Mitch. Sings so pretty, but no song of her own."

"Does she gamble in the club?"

"I hear she does."

"Does she win?"

"I don't know, Mitch," Maye said. "I just don't know."

"Does she lose?"

"Who doesn't?" Maye said matter-of-factly.

"Does she have regular hours?"

"She's in the club now. You know I work in back, but sometimes I get a peek at the customers. She's here on a Saturday night, you can be sure."

"Does she come and go with someone?"

Maye's eyes shone dense as obsidian, flecks of sandstone and mica. She took a long, slow drink of vodka, working the vodka down in gasps.

"You working for the wrong people," she said. "It's none of my affair."

"I'm not working for anyone yet, Maye."

"I don't know who she comes with. It's not her man, that's for sure."

"Do you know what she drives?"

"She drives a purple Hudson. Big car." I scanned the lot for a Hudson. What I saw was an obscure chord of black.

"I got to go, Mr. Roberts. I've had my break and more," Maye said.

"You won't be in trouble?" I asked.

"No, I won't be in any trouble." Maye handed me the vodka. Then she braced herself against the earth and uncorked two thin legs that struggled to rise. I grabbed her hands and we danced for balance. Maye felt frail and light as an old newspaper.

"We'd best go one at a time," I said. "Can you make it down?"

"Yes," she answered. "You not working for the wrong people?"

"I'll watch it."

Maye struggled down the path. Voices seeped from an inky distance like blues from the county jail. I scrambled after Maye and stopped her, holding her silently. The voices intensified, battles of pitch and modulation muffled by a blanket of thicket and dance music.

"Oh, my," Maye said in a hush. "It's Mr. Canard."

I strained my eyes in the blackness. "Which?" I asked.

Maye cupped her hands over her mouth. "The small, hairy one," she whispered.

A black collar bled onto the pink stucco. In the black collar huddled a small spider of a man. He was the size of a Chinese fireplug, solid and subtle as a punch in the face. His bowed arms were covered with a coarse hair, thick wads of it exploding from the white shirt he wore, the wads webbed and coiled as moss on a cypress knob. He wore his hands in his pockets, rocking slowly heel to toe. At the stump of a barrel neck squatted a thick, mushy face, bulbous nose, and bald head. A swath of slick black swaddled the bald head. I smelled the hair with my imagination, pungent as glue and Brylcream. Canard bobbed his head, showing the red trace of cigar arc. Colby swaggered at Canard's elbow, speaking in low tones.

Colby was wearing the same chinos and vest. He leaned against a black Buick, nodding agreement. Canard turned and ascended the outside stairs to his office and disappeared inside a portal above the kitchen entrance. A third shadow floated by Colby.

"Do you know the other two?" I asked Maye.

"Only one," she said.

"The guy in the vest?"

"No. The other one. His name is Nabil Bunch. They call him Bill. He runs the Little River Club up north."

I'd heard of Bunch. He was tall and cast a dense, muscular shadow. In the reputation line, he'd cut ahead of Genghis Khan, just behind Hitler. He was a westside Syrian, dabbler in gambling, prostitution, and booze. His baliwick was a pillbox near the confluence of the Big and Little rivers, a dank, blue-collar cottage with the splendid, old-world charm of a lanced boil. He was head of a gang known as the Indians, a rough bunch of pencil heads known for crooked poker games and striking matches with a thumbnail and a leer. They were a crowd of seedy hoods who did small-time jobs and aspired to big operations but who didn't have the brains or the connections. Once in a blue moon they hit pay dirt, but their cries and whispers didn't carry to the wall.

A door slammed. Canard sauntered down the stone stairs carrying a satchel. He reached the flagstone path and walked to Colby, then handed Colby the satchel. Colby placed it on the hood of the Buick. The three men stood without speaking, embraced by a spiraling corona of shade. Then they spoke, their voices rising and falling in oceanic regularity. Canard puffed his cigar as he rocked, Colby turned to Bunch, and together they walked swiftly to the kitchen and went inside, leaving Canard by himself with silence and cigar smoke.

Maye and I huddled under another blackjack oak, exchanging nervous glances. Maye brought a towel to her face and wiped perspiration from her forehead. Streaks of sweat and flour laced the bony protrusions of her cheeks. Wind collected in the oak crests, droning a nervous rustle like a roomful of office typewriters. A breath of night surrounded the silhouette of Canard, throwing it against the pink stucco of the Canyon Club. The silhouette quivered like a dreamy apparition. Maye held her breath.

"I don't like this," she said. Her breath then came irregularly, with a stertorous hack.

"I'm sorry," I said. We forgot the vodka.

The Syrian cook came out of the kitchen. He emerged swiftly from the glare and passed into shadow. A new figure followed the cook, a paunchy, hunched figure wearing what looked like a blue suit and a felt hat pulled down. The figure shuffled as he walked, wanting to move slowly but not making it. Then came Colby and Bunch, converging behind him. Colby shoved the blue suit.

He staggered into a ring of stares. I strained again into the night, urging my ears to pick up the ring of talk. What emerged was a jumble and clash of unmelodic noise. Clouds moved, and the moon threw a beam on the black car, and the figures noosed around the car in a tight O. Canard puffed smoke into the face of the blue suit. The figures seemed to drift endlessly, movement trickling in unhurried chains like water in an instantaneously dark cavern. My nerves woke up in a rubber room and played dumb. Maye was a rigid spike jabbed to the center of the earth.

Suddenly, Colby twisted behind the blue suit, grabbing him by the hands, cranking the two hands in an arc down and behind. The suited figure staggered in slow motion, arms pinioned in a V rearward. Canard stepped in and grabbed the figure by the hair, knocking off the felt hat. The hat flew. Canard stood, plainly outlined by moonlight, tugging at the lone figure, one hand curled meanly around the back of Blue Suit's neck. Canard bent Blue Suit down, using his hair as a lever, Colby working the man's hands skyward like a pump handle. Together Canard and Colby moved him forward like a sack of jerk-water shit. Bunch moved to the front fender of the Buick and stood, hands on hips. I thought I saw a Cheshire grin smear his dark features. Bunch put a hand on the blue suit's neck; Canard tugged his hair; Colby levered the hands up and back.

The head smacked the fender of the Buick with a shrill crack. It was the sound of sick, dull emptiness; bone, skin, and metal vectored in the certitude of violence. The guy grunted dully, then Bunch and Canard forced his head powerfully toward the fender. Another smack. The guy's legs bucked. He went limp. Colby circled his arms around the guy's waist. Canard released the hair long enough to puff his cigar and tap the ash. Then together Bunch and Canard threw the unconscious man's head against the metal of the Buick. Maye grabbed my arm. The head hit with a clunk and the guy went down.

Maye was gripped by horror. My own mind went blank against the scene, holding itself up stiff-legged and staggering, punch-drunk like a tired fighter in the eighth. I'd seen cruelty before.

Below, Canard extracted a sheet of paper from his pocket, leaned down, and pinned the paper to the lapel of the guy's suit. The three buzzards then lifted the figure and forced him into the backseat of the Buick. Colby picked up his satchel. Bunch entered the Buick and drove it down the gravel drive. Canard turned and entered the club.

Colby stood alone, watching the steady disappearance of the Buick as it descended the curling drive, heading north on Hillside, rising in a steamy drift of headlight and wind.

Colby ambled to the cream and beige Packard and then drove down the same gravel drive.

Maye looked at me. "Mitch Roberts, I didn't want to see that," she said. She closed her eyes wearily.

"Go back to work, Maye. Don't worry."

"What are you going to do?"

"Try to catch the Buick."

Maye stood and began to walk. "You want me to call the police? Can I do that?"

"No, Maye, I'll take care of it."

Maye shook her head. "You'd best hurry then."

Maye scuttled down the slope. She turned.

"Don't you end up like Sonny," she said softly.

I followed Maye, descending the path in the thicket, through scrub oak and sycamore. Rain moved like fate in the south. A thin, quicksilver streak shot through the bruised cloud bank. Maye stood engulfed in white light at the kitchen door, watching me hurry to my car. I touched the starter.

My mind became a hayloft with rats. In the loft a thought formed. We all end like Sonny, it whispered.

FOUR

I forced the Fairlane into a decent trot, skidding down the gravel incline away from the Canyon Club. A wild plume of gravelly mud flared as the tires cornered and gathered speed. I hurdled the culvert and shot past the iron-railed bridge at the bottom of the hill. The odors of black earth and exhaust sailed in. Above the weirdly illumined dash, tracers of dimly outlined taillights jousted with shadows cast by the shacks hugging the shoulders of Hillside. At the telescoped end of night a pair of taillights nosed the steamy embrace of stalled traffic. Another pair floated farther up the hill, fading, reappearing, colliding with the swell of College Hill, faint beacons in a big sea. I settled back for a chase, ignoring the dread that broke into sweat at my brow and seeped out the flannel folds of my collar. I gunned the motor, running on vodka and gasoline.

From a tangle of trees there appeared a clear glimpse of brick street rising along an edge of hill. The hill was a dark thumb, red streaks painted on the nail, traffic extending in dots and dashes along the route. I was lucky. I could see clearly the intersections with side streets. At each, I looked both ways, searching for the black Buick and beige Packard. I ran a stop, screeching around a stumblebum, barely missing a parked Chevy. The stumblebum gave me an obvious message. I didn't blame him. I kissed the vodka, feeling good and clear and cold.

I flipped on the radio and laughed. Patti Page was halfway into "How Much Is That Doggie." Then Hillside swelled between rows of elms and white houses. I pushed the Fairlane to a steady run making my own wind, my line of sight frozen to the hilltop. The narrow street was bathed in whistling shade, porch lamps streamed together in a gauzy haze. Finally, I saw the beige Packard down a side street, stopped at a light. Colby was slouched at the wheel, smoking, feathering smoke through the window into night. He didn't look back and he had no one in the car with him. The signal changed and he wheeled the big Packard south and disappeared in a hurry for nothing. Colby was on his route back to the Black Fox Ranch. I had it figured that the satchel contained the week's receipts and the books and records of the Canyon. It made sense to start over at midnight on Saturday.

I gunned the Fairlane again, descending the hill, my sight fixed on Arcturus in the sky. There was another red light far away. I hoped it was the taillight of a big, black car edging into Uptown. I hoped the big, black car was in no hurry.

The vodka kissed back. It slid a silver tongue down into my belly and sucked. I wanted a gun.

I sideswiped a stroller and his dog, beating a red light. I contemplated the fate of the guy in the blue suit. A sense of fear joined the vodka in my belly. Maye and I had not witnessed the slow-motion nosedive of a drunk. I'd seen drunks stiffed before, hauled out by beefy guys in vests, kicked in the pants, and left in a ditch. There was nothing elaborate or enjoyable about it, and bouncers took no particular pleasure in their work. I could see guys like Bunch and Canard having fun with a stiff, but I couldn't see the ceremony, the attention to detail, the loving care, being wasted on a drunk on Saturday night in the parking lot behind the club. It didn't make sense. I knew, too, that the westside Indians were mean. They burned puppies and laid odds on the weight of the ashes. There was the story of a drifter who woke with ten fingers nailed to a telephone pole. He'd tried to swipe a case of hootch from the Little River Club. It was the sort of story that created a stir on prayer night at the Baptist church. There had been something else about this scene. Something else, indeed.

There was Colby. If the guy in the blue suit was just another drunk, then Colby didn't make sense. He didn't fit. He was a first sacker with a catcher's mitt. You'd think that the snot-nosed Syrian could have thrown Blue Suit in a ditch all by himself. But the scene had had all the contenders dancing for the title, everybody having fun bouncing the guy's head on metal. It was too much for too little, and it didn't make sense.

Then there was the note. Canard had pinned a note to the guy's chest. Cruising uphill, I lit a cigarette and knew that it was the note I wanted to see. I wanted to see the note before the police.

I caught the Buick in Uptown. Uptown is a slice of the city filled with bars, cinemas, pool halls, and liquor stores. There is a Lutheran church and Catholic church and a place that rents crutches and party supplies. A Rexall Drug sells sodas. The black Buick idled at the corner. A huddle of snooker players hunched in thin light, drinking beer, sucking the last of their whiskey, waiting to go home, crawling downhill into sleep. Beer signs flickered. In the moth-filled glare I saw Bunch behind the wheel and the dark shape of another man in back.

I slowed the Fairlane, politely staying behind. Bunch drove deliberately. The street widened, passing a gloomy hospital, running north into maple and elm. At Ninth Street, Bunch rumbled over the tracks and into the north end. I tossed the vodka. I stayed behind by two blocks, confident that the Buick was an easy target in the dark, deserted streets. Those guys were looking for no one. It's a way to be followed, looking for no one. It came upon me that Bunch wasn't going to kill the guy in the blue suit. There had been too many quick ways into the country, fast exits to dark lanes where they could pike the guy and dump him. If Bunch was going to pike the guy, he would have headed east, into the country.

I lit a cigarette. The smoke clawed a hole to my heart, shredding tissue. Bunch turned north and circled old Maple Grove Cemetery. Maple Grove was a forty-acre necropolis: big mausoleums, stones, monuments, and bric-a-brac shrouded in a thick network of maple and old, red cedar. The place was spooky as a blind date. In fall, I'd walk in the cold and dark, eyeing crows, reading the old tombstones, savoring the violent loneliness, regarding the murky stillness as a private confine. I knew the paths well.

Bunch parked the Buick on a side street. I idled to a stop down the street and clicked the lights. The two men carried Blue Suit into the black mouth of Maple Grove. I shuddered. There had been vodka in the bottle when I tossed it.

I slithered from the Fairlane and opened the trunk. I took off my tweeds and hauled on a denim jacket I kept for fishing. I leaned into the car for a flash, then crossed the street and skirted a stone fence in front of the toolshed. Maple Grove was an earthquake of sound. Night birds whipped. Starlings cackled. The silken maple leaves rustled like crinoline. I peeked, then slipped into the same black mouth.

I rested in the shadow of a stone. A holy couple and one sheep looked down. I waited. In the night, I could see Bunch meander among tombstones and monuments, grunting, the two forms moving like fish in the wreckage of a forlorn galleon. Bunch moved his flash in the maple shade, then stopped. There was no movement then, only the sound of hushed labor, the shuffle of shoes on cedar needles. A few lonely crows flew. The night stayed dark. I wanted a smoke. Acres of darkness away, a few cars cruised on Hillside, their misty headlights dusting the stone flanks of the cemetery.

I moved to the folds of an old cedar. Forty acres of Maple Grove exhaled in the solemn embrace of wind. Bunch and his sidekick carried Blue Suit in a stuttered gait, both stopping to huff and puff. Blue Suit sagged, arms and legs flopping in a rag-mop X. Bunch clicked the flash and again a solid beam exploded onto primitive shapes arranged in ritual symmetry. My flesh folded and crept away. In the instantaneous glare I watched Bunch and his sidekick working, their voices eroded by the dark and the distance. The other man was short and the shape of an oak barrel, his snap brim low. For a while they didn't speak. Then they stopped working and walked quickly to a graveled lane, went along it quietly, and then went back out the dark mouth of the cemetery.

I waited as the black Buick drove away. Moonlight moved in the moving clouds. A silver curtain descended.

Blue Suit was on his back, tied to a stone slab. His suit hung around him like bad news. There was a pure look of cherubic unconsciousness on his fat face. The face was ruddy, two black eyebrows pressing rheumy eyes like upturned parentheses. He had too much double chin for a guy twenty-five years old. I leaned into his face.

There was a noose around the guy's neck. It was a nice noose tied in a thunderous budweiser, tight as a salesman's daughter. The other end was tied to a brass ring on the ornate end of a concrete flower pot. Another noose bound the guy's legs. The loose end led to grillwork on a mausoleum door.

I took a chance and looked the guy over with the flash. His hands were bound at his sides. With luck, he could get loose in about ten days if the crows didn't get him first. The chubby face cradled a pug nose pushed back into his face. It was an innocent face, smooth as a beach ball. He had a thick mop of brown hair lying in a curly mass around pugnacious ears. I pushed back the mop and eyed the bruise.

It was a beauty. A faint yellow cesspool the size of a half dollar veined by black threads and blue mice. The guy's heart was beating. I took that for a good sign. In the shallows, breath came in twos, weak and steady as a two-diamond bid. He was out and he was hurt. He wasn't going to die. He wouldn't multiply from memory again, but he wasn't going to die.

I jerked the wallet out of his back pocket. The guy was Charlie Allison. There were two hundred dollars in the wallet, a Kansas driver's license, a Social Security card, a pack of cheap condoms, a spare house key, and a few scraps of paper with phone numbers. A card read: Please accept this card as a token of my deepest sympathy. Some jokester. I put back the wallet and didn't take any of the money. I lit a cigarette.

I leaned on the slab. I pushed the round halo of flash on the note pinned to the guy's chest. It was a nice note. Not as nice as the noose, not as nice as the bruise, but a nice note. NEXT TIME THIS YAKKER GOES UNDER-GROUND, it said. I thought that was clear enough.

I figured to drive home and call the police. I'd give them the tip and hang up. I didn't want to waltz around the station house with a fat sergeant who'd probably step on my lovely head. In that time the crows wouldn't eat Charlie Allison. I hustled down the gravel lane and away from the slab. A musty cedar smell floated through the night. I felt uncertain and confused but didn't know exactly why.

I heard the dark car as I approached the front gate. It crunched along a gravel road that entered the cemetery from behind, near the caretaker's cottage and stone warehouse shed. Tires made a muffled hush on the gravel. It drove slowly, splitting a huge dark monument with light, sliding past a cedar copse, two beams outlined there briefly until the lights were extinguished. I ducked. The car stopped and a form emerged. A funnel of light hissed past me when a flashlight popped on. The spotlight darted like a moth. There was a question. I decided it was about me.

I broke. A voice behind me carved a stop sign. I didn't stop. I hopped the stone fence and ran, stooping, crazy with cold vodka boiling my blood. What I heard then, I'd heard before, plenty. If you've never heard it, you don't know. There is almost no use telling about it. The sound is like a metal bee, tumbling and dangerous and fast. It whanged above my head, solid and memorable. My mind and muscles cinched themselves tightly against the rush. I ran. When I reached the Fairlane, I hit the starter. There wasn't another whang. At least I didn't hear one.

Ninth Street disappeared and I was in a neighborhood maze, quiet and respectable. I listened for sirens and heard nothing. I didn't look back. I slowed the car and emerged into the semibrightness of Hillside going south. Black cars and bullets tinkled in my brain like spare change. In Uptown the bars and honky-tonks were quiet. A few guys waltzed lampposts. My fear eased and I began to think.

It wasn't a cop. Maye hadn't called them. No cop could have followed that closely. Besides, the dark car that pulled into the cemetery went right to the spot like it had a map. I knew the guy wasn't a cop because no cop would take a public, wild shot at a shadow. A thug might open fire because he had nothing to lose, though. Thugs didn't mind those things. One thing was certain. Bunch and Canard and Colby had tagged the guy with a note on his blue suit's lapel so that someone would be sure to read it when Charlie Allison surfaced in the morning. The second guy was a little nervous and a lot angry. It explained the wild shot.

I pulled onto Sycamore, hoping that there was muscatel at home. I drove through the dark alley behind my house and parked in the spot beside the rabbits. The big house was dark, cavernous, and creaky. I went up the back steps and into the kitchen, catching the odor of dust and old bacon grease and lilacs in bloom. Big Ben muttered twelve-thirty and I relaxed. It turned out that there was a new gallon of muscatel under the sink.

I walked a tumbler of it to the front porch. The night had cleared. Across Sycamore, a bank of lights glowed in the ballpark. Groundskeepers swept trash from dark ticket booths. One or two cars remained in the parking lot. Otherwise, the darkness held a silence as thick as pitch. I sat in my rocking chair and looked at Christine asleep on the porch rail, one shoulder balanced by a strut, her curly head nuzzled on an ample bosom. She snored softly, a gentle calliope sound. I nudged her awake.

"Oh, hi," she said. She yawned.

Christine was a regular Orphan Annie: big saucer eyes, freckled face, lush lips. She could smile open vaults, melt lead, blackmail nations.

"Hello," I said back. Christine played the organ for the Braves during the baseball season. In the evenings I'd sneak into the park in the late innings and watch the game for free. I'd sit in the darkened grandstand and bring Christine beer between innings. When her loneliness was great, she'd drift over after the game to smoke and to drink muscatel. I knew nothing of Christine except that her brown hair smelled of wild sage and that her skin was soft as a lonely beach. I smiled at her.

"It's ball season," she said with a grin. She pulled her knees under her chin. She had on a bulky wool sweater, jeans, and cowboy boots. She always did.

"So it is," I said. We'd had this conversation before.

"The Braves won. They slaughtered Indianapolis. We had a good crowd. I got a little drunk and came over. Is it all right?"

"Of course," I replied. "But you know. I don't know a thing about you."

"I know about you, though. You live alone and you think too much." Christine reached for the muscatel. I handed her the glass and she drank. She slid from the rail and sat on my knee. "You look tired," she said.

"I am. I've been on the move since morning. There's a problem I haven't worked out yet. Scrambled brain."

"And you want to talk," she said. A ticket taker entered his old Chevy, then lumbered the dead pistons up Sycamore. He twisted the car through a wheel of exhaust fume and went away. Christine nuzzled her hair in my face. She felt warm and sleepy. "So we'll talk about ourselves. You first."

I shook my head and drank muscatel.

"Yes, you first," said Christine. "Mother?"

"All right. Lives on a farm with my grandma. They do fine. I visit the farm and rest."

"Brothers and sisters?"

"None I've been told about."

"Father?"

"Dead as Millard Fillmore."

"Who's Millard Fillmore?" asked Christine. There was a look of genuine dismay crowding her drowsy smile.

"He's just dead. That's all."

"Tell me about him. How'd he die?" I drank some musky. For me the past was a fat teacher in the first grade mapping a solid course of failure and repression; a buddy dead on Omaha Beach, his arms waving in the surf. The past was a kiss in the coat closet; women crying. Gravity, superego, and Freud bowdlerized for the masses. I got schmaltzy thinking about the past. I gulped and started.

"My old man died when I was a kid. Son of a bitch didn't have the decency to hang around to teach me about hitting curve balls. Or anything else. I was three days old when he died. I think that if he had been around I would be playing third base in Double AA ball. I'd have had a good life, riding the bus to Springfield and Joplin, watching guys with talent move up to Triple AAA. In winter, I'd be working in the dusty general store in Altamont, holding on until April when spring training opened."

"You sure sound sorry for yourself," Christine said. Another thing about Christine. She sometimes scored a bull's-eye on the bullshit.

"Is that what it is?"

"Maybe, Mitch."

"Then let's say it is. I feel sorry for the whole busload of us. I just want to play third base and leave the thinking to Republicans."

Christine put an arm around my neck. I smelled sage. "So what about your father," she said.

"To hear tell, my mother was in the hospital in Parsons letting the stitches heal, trying to figure what kind of monster she had just birthed. On the outside, my old man decides to head to Cherryvale to the drive-in movie.

"He took his buddy, Omer Throckmorton, and a couple of girls who were cheerleaders. They took a fifth of bourbon under a blanket in the backseat. It was a hell of a night, drinking whiskey, playing radio, copping feels of the girls. It was late, the cartoon and the news played a second time. Omer and his girlfriend listened to the radio for two hours with the ignition off, so when my old man started the car the battery was dead. Omer poured some whiskey in the carburetor, then the both of them rolled the Chevy from its perch at the drive-in, down the lane, and through the front gate. They pushed the car down a hill, the girls urging them on. The girls were afraid and they had to get home. They probably thought the dead battery was a trick hatched by Omer and my dad. The Chevy finally turned over and off they went down the highway, singing and drinking whiskey.

"It was bright, a moonlit night. You could see down the highway for miles, the highway a glimmering ribbon. Sunflowers danced in the wind. You could smell the oats and the hay. My old man drove, and he decided then and there to drive all the way home with the lights out to save juice.

"Omer tells it yet. My old man was in the middle of a sentence. The two girls were singing. They hit a turnip farmer's truck head-on in the moonlight. Omer says they hit smack. The whole car filled with dust, flying glass, and steam. Sounds roared and died. When it was silent, Omer got out the back door and started running. He was so scared he ran a mile through a field, then stopped and sat in a corn row and smoked a cigarette. Then he went back to the car.

"Everybody was on the road except my old man. The old farmer was sitting in his britches, crying. The girls were covered with dust and blood. The truck had flipped a load of turnips into the Chevy through the busted front window. My old man was inside the car, covered with turnips.

"Omer and the farmer got into the car. My old man had one hand on the wheel. Omer says he didn't finish his last sentence, but he looked like he was ready. Omer remembers my old man saying, 'Jesus Christ, Omer,' he said, 'you know what I got in my right hand?' That was it. The girls cried and screamed. Omer and the farmer dug my old man out of the turnips and took a look.

"My old man sat bolt upright looking pleased and a little drunk, smiling at what he had in his right hand. There was a drop of blood on his lip. It had dripped from his nose. On his temple was a gray-blue bruise. He was dead as a mackerel.

"I went to the funeral on my mother's tit. My old man looked fine in his powder-blue suit, pink tie. His black hair was slicked and wavy. My mother was sixteen then. She raised me with the help of my grandma. I went to war, found out about muscatel, and it's been downhill ever since."

Christine said, "You're funny." Then we went to bed

and started ball season. Later I smoked while she slept, the small calliope notes seeping from her sleep. I thought about graveyards and cops and bullets, but I couldn't sleep.

I left the bed and sat in the gray overstuffed chair, thinking, playing chess, and smoking. In the utter silence of Sunday morning, surrounded by smoke and the lambent swath of lamplight, I studied a game played by Lasker in Berlin. It was a small, desperate game, serpentine, wriggling an idea to the core of unmeaning. In the end, Lasker won as he usually did.

I drank most of the muscatel. Sometime in the night, Christine woke, kissed me, and left the old house. By dawn I was drunk and ready to take Reynard's ten thousand.

FIVE

Woolly worms sparred speed rounds and worked the heavy bags of my eyelids. Ogres marched to college fight songs along the swollen course of my inner ear. Hannibal and his elephants practiced pirouettes in my gullet. What must have been a Moorish caravan dumped campfire ashes down my throat.

It was a bad night. I woke bolt upright in the gray over-stuffed chair, my clothes sweating like a decent lightweight in the fifth round. I wiggled my right hand. It was there, curled delicately around the muscatel jug. Neon festooned my brain, moths soared on brittle wings, and a thin film of diseased dust collapsed against my scalp. I popped another eyelid open and recoiled from the pearly beauty of spring.

A meow tinkled. Francis sat stirring his fuzz noisily on my lap. He ran a pink tongue along a foreleg and allowed the tongue to lick some crusty skin on my right thumb. I sat squashed inside a thread of sunlight, distinctly fiery as it fell on the nuts and bolts of my skeleton. Francis hopped onto the arm of the chair and cast a crooked and sardonic glare onto my face. Through the open front door a thousand sounds clamored, elms rushed in the wind, squirrels darted and dashed in the green embrace of limbs, honks and toots and chugs of people driving by erupted. There was the unmistakable *plop* of baseball bat and horsehide.

Some people lived and kicked. I was unlikely to live. The Big Ben on my bedside table said one o'clock. The book of Lasker's games lay open on my lap and the dismembered shreds of Latakia littered my knees. Muscle popped and a thought emerged. I came alive slowly like a mile-long freight moving up Pike's Peak. Forty thousand reasons to die raised their hands. A big, sweaty eunuch smashed a lambswool hammer into a brass plate. I moved upward, feeling my clothes break against me like painted cardboard.

There was too much sun and too much noise and too much animal hoopla for a man who'd drunk the better part of a gallon of muscatel. I hobbled to the shower like a vet from Belleau Wood.

I melted in the hot water. A head appeared like a poached peach. I located a pair of hands and used them to wash the night and the liquor away. I shaved. My face resembled nine miles of chuckholes on a county road. I reached from the shower and flipped on the one-thirty news. There was nothing in five minutes about Charlie Allison and the Maple Grove Cemetery. There were stories about car crashes, plane crashes, and political skullduggery, but nothing about a fat, little man hogtied to a cement slab in a dark cemetery. Nothing about the note, nothing about nothing.

For a time the lack of news didn't bother me. I was more worried about a face smooth as a red ant heap. I felt an indistinct hunger, got out of the shower, and dressed in clean slacks, dark blue dress shirt, and my grandpa's fancy brown vest. When I stepped from the bathroom, I saw Andy Lanham standing beside the oak table, smiling, his head bobbing amid the dead cacti.

Andy was a lieutenant in Homicide at the Wichita P.D. We'd been friends since we'd returned from the war, both of us struggling to collate the pieces of discombobulated lives. So far, he had picked up most of his pieces. He owned a wife, two kids, and a steady job. Our lives mingled in the piecemeal structure of baseball games, chess, and philosophical uncertainty in shades of gray. In the war of nerves against life, we were vaguely on the same team.

Andy was big and red as a beach ball, slate freckles sprinkled randomly on a wide-angle face, hair stealing a lopsided embrace around copper ears. His hands were all knuckles.

He slid around the table. ''You look like a hunk of spoiled pork,'' he said.

''Spoiled pork has a reason to live.''

Andy held a teak, Staunton king from my set. In the big room to one side his two kids bounced on my brass bed. They were five-year-old Tinkertoys, towheaded and freckled as a case of measles. They bounced like airy muffins and giggled. Andy tossed the king from hand to hand, eyeing me.

''Game starts in fifteen minutes,'' he said. Andy looked at the Tinkertoys. They bounced.

''Oh, shit,'' I replied. I remembered a two o'clock date with Andy to go to the minor league game on Sunday.

''We slaughtered Indianapolis last night,'' Andy said.

I went to the kitchen and he followed. I made coffee and returned to the alcove. We sat down at the oak table. The twins played with Francis. Andy and I sipped coffee in the sun.

''You ever heard of a guy named Charlie Allison?'' I asked Andy.

Andy put down the coffee and cupped his hands under the base of his chin. ''For Christ sake,'' he said. ''You're not working again this soon after the trial?''

Andv had shepherded me through the trial. I knew he hoped it was over and that I'd get some decent job pushing aircraft parts along a conveyor belt and find myself a little platinum number with bluebells for a smile. He wanted me in a life of somber necessity.

He sighed. "Never heard of Charlie Allison in my life," he said.

"When you were in Vice, did you ever run into Gus Canard or a guy named Bunch?"

"I'm a cop," Andy answered. "Cops live in the same world as everybody else. Is this interrogation strictly necessary?"

Andy had been a vice cop for four long years. He'd slipped his bonds and found himself in Homicide. I knew he didn't want to remember the bad old days. Since leaving Vice he felt better about himself and his life. These memories were belches in his psyche.

"Just tell me how it works with the Canyon Club and the Little River. That's all I want to know."

Andy stood and hitched his belt.

"The cops in Vice aren't strictly on the take, if that's what you want to know. There are plenty of clubs around town, big and small. They make contributions to the reelection of the D.A. The D.A. makes contributions to the reelection of the governor. The governor has a blind eye and attends church. I don't know where the money goes, but vice cops keep their jobs by being blind. At Christmas they take home a little extra. Sometimes there's a rogue who shakes down the club owner all by himself. It happens."

Blindness trickled like blood in a syringe. I stiffened the question.

"Do you know Bunch and Canard?"

"Creeping crud, Mitch. Out of Kansas City. They've been on the scene so long they think they own the town. It's guys like that who make the payments. When I was in Vice, they left me alone. I think they knew I didn't go along with the deal. As long as Canard and Bunch pay their dues, the D.A. doesn't prosecute." Andy lit a cigar. "They've been working like that since the thirties."

"What about Jules Reynard?"

"Same deal. Higher class than most. Not like Bunch. He's one of the westside Indians. Bunch is a mushy cantelope. Nobody likes that."

"Know a guy named Colby?"

"No," Andy said. "But I'll tell you. This year the shit could hit the fan. There's a hot governor's race and if the Democrats come in, they could come in on a reform ticket. You know there's a new liquor bill before the legislature making a drink easier. You might see six months from now the end of gambling and the beginning of a shot of whiskey in a bar."

The kids developed ominous silence at the window in my front room. Mischief grew like mushrooms in the basement. One of the Tinkertoys had Francis by the tail. Francis persevered.

"Who makes the physical payment of cash?" I asked.

"Reynard and Bunch, I suppose. Nobody else runs gambling with those guys."

"Could you check out Charlie Allison for me? I think some of the boys punched him out last night. There should be a police report. If there isn't, then something is fishy."

"You coming to the game or not?" said Andy.

"I can't."

"Last week you moaned about how we never see each other."

The Tinkertoys built themselves into a pretzel and overturned the jug of musky. Green dribbled to the burnished floor. Andy and I looked at them. They gave back an it-wasn't-our-fault expression.

"Make some calls for me?" Andy shook his head in consternation. "I'll meet you at the pond tonight at six o'clock. We can fish together and talk this over. Just dig up something about Allison. I'd appreciate it."

"Goddamnit," Andy said. "I'm not a vice cop. I can't afford to nose around in their business." Andy stared at his shoes. Finally he said, "All right, goddamnit. I wish we weren't friends and I wish you'd go back to serving subpoenas and sneaking into the last three innings of ball games."

"Vote for Stevenson. Country will shape up."

"My ass," said Andy. He smiled, but it came from a place far away, from a place Andy had left and didn't want to see again. Andy's road held family, kids, and apple pie. Mine was detours and dirt.

Andy spoke. "See you at the pond. Six o'clock. Be there and bring me a cigar. I'll bring a six-pack from home."

Andy towed the Tinkertoys through the front screen. They crossed Sycamore and joined the crowd at the ballpark. I phoned Reynard and told him I'd be out to the Black Fox in thirty minutes. He said he'd be expecting me. He didn't say anything about Charlie Allison.

I drove the highway to Black Fox Ranch. A cobalt sky arched gloriously, dotted by puffy white clouds. Lilac and honeysuckle seeped, blackbirds, whippoorwills, and meadowlarks played on the prairie. It was a delicious day, nice enough to make ten thousand dollars out of nothing. I drove the gravel drive beside the horse pasture. The horses gamboled. I parked in the pine copse and pounded on the big door. Reynard opened the door, Tiresias at his side.

"It's me," I said. Reynard led me to the flagstone porch. We sat at an iron table in the sunshine. Below us, the horseshoe lake dimpled and dappled in a gentle breeze. A few bass jumped in the reeds.

"I'll take your offer," I said.

Reynard wore seersucker pants and a Banlon shirt. He poured iced tea and we drank. I belched muscatel on top of no breakfast.

"I have the cash in the house. I'll get it when you're ready to leave."

"What about the job at the Canyon?" I asked.

"It's arranged. Gus Canard is expecting you to drop around sometime tonight. He won't ask too many questions. I let him think you're out of Kansas City, some punk being put on the payroll."

"What's my name?"

"Use your own. Canard hasn't read anything but a racing form in fifteen years."

I sipped some iced tea.

"What about Agnes?" I asked Reynard.

He was silent. In the windy reeds, red-winged blackbirds dipsydoodled. The air gathered smells: fresh prairie hay, alfalfa, ripening wheat, horses. A string of redbuds were south of the horse pasture, a red gash on green fields.

Agnes hadn't caused a flinch. Reynard's eyes were needle-solid on nothingness. He seemed to me a man adrift on a burning ship, hopeless and far from landfall. If he was right and his wife was with another man, then I could only surmise at his capacity to inflict revenge. I decided I wouldn't think about it.

"You'll run into Agnes at the club," Reynard said. "It won't take long and you can't miss her."

I lit a Lucky, then helped Reynard with one of his black cigars. We smoked.

"The horses that died," I said. "How many, how old?"

"Yearlings. There were two. Colby found them one morning on the back section."

"What was done with them?"

"What do you mean?"

"How did you dispose of them?"

"Colby took care of that. I suppose our vet did the messy work. I don't really know. He's a fellow named Glick, in Augusta."

"You didn't handle it?"

"I was in the hospital. I could barely hold down the lime Jell-O."

"You ever heard of a guy named Charlie Allison?" I asked Reynard.

"Never," he answered. "Should I?"

"I'll get back to you," I said, and rose.

"Don't hold out on me," said Reynard. Tiresias gathered himself and stood. I tried to detect the motion from Reynard that controlled the dog, but it was subtle enough to slip by me. I still didn't like the looks of all those sharp white teeth in the dog's face. A pair of swans went by.

"You called Canard about the job. I guess that means you were sure I'd take your money," I said.

Reynard seemed to be studying something with his mind's eye. Tiresias stayed stock-still.

"I'm a gambler," he said at last. "The odds looked pretty good."

We walked toward the house. "What's your relationship to Bunch?" I asked.

"He's a hood. I don't have any relationship to hoods."

"Not now?"

"Ever," said Reynard. He said it loud.

"Anybody else I should look out for?"

"You'll run into my son," he said. I looked for Colby in the house. I saw no one.

"What about your son?"

"I set him up in a little racket over on West Douglas. It's a pony shop; you've probably been there once or twice. Ten folding chairs, a wire window, twenty telephones. You can get down on half a dozen tracks. It's a cracker-and-soda operation. Guy bets two bucks every forty minutes. Some deal. My son is not what you'd call executive material. He drinks too much and he's flashy."

"I suppose I'll run into him?"

"You'll see him at the Canyon. He loses money in my club to impress the ladies. He's twenty-five years old and has the morals of a tomcat. My first wife has been dead a long time, Mr. Roberts. I don't remember how he happened."

The sunshine turned cold. "These horses that were killed," I said. "Were they broke?"

Reynard doused his cigar in a silver ashtray. "I used to break some of the horses. Since my blindness, the horses are sold unbroke. The two that were killed would have been sold this summer."

"Colby doesn't break them?"

"Colby couldn't break toast with a hammer. He's out of Kansas City. He runs errands, does the books. You might say he's more my bodyguard than anything else. He works the dogs."

"You kept the horses on a section?"

"The pasture is a whole section. Six hundred acres." We paused in the sun. "Look," said Reynard. "If you think you can work back from the horses to the people who skim at my club, you're ass backwards. I'm sure there's a connection, but wouldn't it be just as easy to spot the skimming and let the horses take care of themselves?"

"Just curious," I said.

We went into the main room of the ranch. By day the place was not a mysterious sanctum of shadow and shade. There were still two zebra couches, plush chairs, and an onyx chess set. There were still a wicker bar and shiny bottles, still the wet smell of palm from the conservatory. But in sunshine and wind, the big room seemed empty and lifeless. Sounds were sucked away. We sat on the couches.

"I've been studying the game," Reynard said. "With my hands."

Reynard fingered a rook. "I think that last pawn move of yours was a mistake." He moved a bishop, capturing a pawn. We played a few slow moves. I forced a knight to the corner. I still tried to confuse Reynard with wild, ambiguous moves. Later, I hopped a knight into another corner.

"Time out," Reynard said. "Let's take this up again when I've had some time to analyze."

Tiresias led him to a Klee reproduction above a big philodendron. Reynard moved the picture and fiddled with a combination safe. He returned and handed me a bundle of bills. My heart thudded.

"Isn't this where I say count it and you say there's no need for that?" Reynard said. He smiled. It was a salty smile.

"I'll count it at home," I said.

We walked slowly to the big door. I turned. "Where does Agnes stay in town?" I asked.

"There's a single-story Tudor across from the golf course in Sleepy Hollow. Looks like gingerbread and poison ivy. Are you thinking about staking it out?"

"Just thinking for now," I said. "I'll let you know." I went through the door into the sunshine. I drove away looking for Colby, but I didn't see a thing. I had a cold shiver, brought on by easy money.

At home I changed into jeans and boots. I went into the backyard and dug five holes and filled the holes with rabbit shit. I planted tomatoes and built two cucumber hills and staked a dozen green pepper plants. Mrs. Thompson hobbled down her rickety stairs and joined me. I dug and she watered with an old coffee can. By July, we'd be sharing fresh vegetables from the garden. In those hot days I'd sit on the back porch, drinking muscatel and listening to the ball game, the summer thick as soup, the fireflies bright dots. Mrs. Thompson would be by my side and we'd eat fresh tomatoes and watch the sky turn to gold, mauve, and black. I put in two hills of squash and then stopped.

I washed, then left for the pond to meet Andy. I drove north into the countryside. The sky had turned fuzzy pink, flowing like a woman's scarf. Wind kissed the cottonwoods, and in the creek bottoms cattails jingled. Green pasture, corn, milo, and endless whirling wheat painted the land. Cows grazed dells. Along a hedgerow I saw Andy's car and stopped. From the Fairlane I spotted him beneath a big cottonwood. He was casting a shiny lure into turquoise water. The water glittered, a necklace of precious stones. I hefted my tackle from the trunk and hiked across pasture and hopped barbed-wire fences. Andy smiled and casted. There was a can of beer at his feet, propped against a fallen trunk on a mud-and-sand bank. Andy rested one foot on the trunk. The air had cooled, and the hawks, kites, and bats swooped.

"I got a big one before you got here." Andy laughed. "Five-pounder."

"You bet," I said. "Size of a boxcar, no doubt." I shook a spinner free from the tackle box, tied it to the line, and shot the lure into the gloaming. It splashed into a circle of sunbeams. I pulled it home. We fished in silence, circling the pond in opposite directions. I watched Andy pull a small bass to the bank and release it.

"Monster," he mouthed. "Noah should be so lucky."

We fished for an hour, pulling in small bass, releasing them. We met at the cottonwood, popped beers, and drank quietly. I smoked. A dozen Angus gathered at the shallow end of the pond and drank. Evening nested in the gold cottonwoods. The pond was filled by fish circles.

"The lunkers are too smart for us," Andy said.

"Who won the game?"

"Braves, who else? Hot damn, they've got a good team. Hell, those guys could be major leaguers." We finished the beers and stowed the tackle. Stars twinkled in the velvet sky. A few horses joined the cows to drink.

"I have to ask you something, Mitch," Andy said. "It's serious. I need to know."

"I'll try," I said.

"What's between you and Charlie Allison?"

"Just casual sex," I said with a smile.

"I'm serious," Andy said. Nothing in his look made me think otherwise.

"I don't know a damn thing about Charlie Allison. Never spoke to him in my life. Honest."

"Why did you ask about him? What's going down?"

We hiked uphill through the pasture. In places, the bluestem was knee-deep. A flinty moon wove shadows along a spine of prairie.

"This is square, Andy," I said. "He may have something to do with a case I'm working. I don't know Allison, never met him, and don't know what he's up to. It's just a hunch I'm playing, that's all. I have a reason for asking, but I don't know. I can't tell you about the client, you know that."

Andy lit a cigar. He chewed the end and stared into distances that were dark. Miles away, trucks lumbered down a slice of highway, headlights wavering, sounds of gears and engines like rhino in the bush.

"Look, Mitch," Andy said. "The boys who run clubs have been paying off a long time. This election is going to see a lot of dirty politics. For now, they pay the D.A. and he pays the governor, and everybody stays happy and elected. When I was in Vice, every cop knew and kept quiet and did his job, no questions asked. These days, somebody is rocking the boat."

"What about Allison?" I asked.

"I don't know, Mitch. This Allison is twenty-four years old, just out of law school. He's some kind of runner for the Democratic candidate. They're the outsiders, you know."

Andy slid his rod into the backseat of his Chevy and put the tackle box in the trunk. He relit his dead cigar, stuck it into his mouth, and leaned his big frame against the car roof.

"What the hell is this all about?" I asked.

"Early this morning two guys were fishing off the bridge along the Little River confluence. They found Allison face-down in the mud, hands tied behind his back. He'd been thrown off the bridge. He was unconscious when he hit, and he drowned. He's as dead as you can get."

Cold hands caressed me, purple lips brushed my cheek.

The air was suddenly bone-dry, drained of starshine and moonglow. The flinty moon became a death's head.

"We'll talk about this," Andy said. He got into the Chevy and drove away. I watched the red taillights disappear down the country road, powdery dust rising like mist behind him as he went.

SIX

Storms brooded south and east. Slate-colored shafts dropped onto the prairie. In the liquid distances, waving wheat, milo, sorghum, and corn drew a thatched weave onto the land. Clouds hung like bloody plums above the luminescent shape of a grain elevator, the shape itself a vibrant white hulk. Birds scurried for cover through wind dense with dust and ozone. I drove the Fairlane along a dark bandage of highway and into the pink underbelly of sunset, the highway rising and falling like a heartbeat. My own heart beat rhythmically with fear.

I saw the face of Charlie Allison on a stone slab, fat and pink and cheery, sleep and breath stealing silently through his body. In my mind I saw his face again, this time stone-white against aluminum: a face illumined by the glare of a surgeon's lamp, scalpel peeling scales of skull, hammer crushing bone, inside his head a mushy, gray brain veined with red. I'd seen autopsies and heard the cheerful banter of the doctor as he broke skin, sawed bone. Along the horizon, a powerful rumble broke. I couldn't guess the vortex that had caused Allison's death, couldn't control my feelings of responsibility and guilt for it. I tried to conclude that weariness alone had made me take the ten thousand dollars. I felt like using the money to buy a rowboat, then rowing the boat to Tahiti. And staying there.

Allison had been alive at midnight Saturday. By morning on Sunday, he was fish bait on the Little River, staring bug-eyed into six feet of wet mud. I needed to think about motive and opportunity and all the stuff you read about in Agatha Christie. Whoever had killed him had known where to find Charlie Allison in Maple Grove and had done it to achieve a theatrical effect. It could have been the work of one of the Indians, but it had to be someone connected with the mob and the clubs. I lit a smoke and tore the Fairlane through twilight thick as chowder. My mouth was dirt dry. The smoke didn't help that. Nothing would help that.

The killer had been minutes behind me. He drove a big car and knew Maple Grove. It didn't seem likely that it could have been Bunch and his buddy in the Buick. I'd seen Colby leave, but he was a lone driver in a big car. Canard was unaccounted for, but so were dozens of other connected punks. The Syrian cook. Anyone.

I whirled into the alley behind my house and drove by the rabbits and chickens, then parked beside the old carriage house and shed. Mrs. Thompson stood on the upstairs veranda, her wobbly vision on waves of crows heading to the rich grain north and west of town. They'd rest and feed and nest. Mrs. Thompson, like me, couldn't sleep. The waves of crows drove against the steady south wind and the storms drove east. You could smell rain that would strike grass somewhere. I waved to Mrs. Thompson and went inside the old house. I drank some muscatel.

I began to think. Christine was right; I thought too much. This time, I conjured a vision of Canard and Colby and Bunch popping Allison's head hard against metal and felt the concussion of skin and bone, heard Allison's grunt. I imagined a form dragging Allison to the bridge rail and dropping him the fifteen feet. Then Allison was gone, pressed into the fetid blackness, asleep forever.

I changed clothes in the dark. I wore some clean wool

slacks, a flannel shirt, a pair of tan oxfords, and a tweed sport coat. I combed my locks and washed old shreds of hair from the comb. With luck, I'd last until forty. As it was, I felt my liver and kidneys cringing in the basement of my gut, waiting for more muscatel.

I drove to the Canyon Club. It was a quiet, glowing ark. There were a few cars in the parking lot. Soft music washed the night. One of the Syrian cooks leaned against the kitchen door smoking. He was the same dark man with hairy arms I'd seen the night before. He had the same unemotional stare. I stubbed my smoke and walked the stone steps to the pink portico of the club. Green palms dipped into a Moorish entry. I went inside.

Pale light bubbled. I stopped in the entry and looked back at the parking lot. There was a huge, burgundy Hudson parked in shadow, unlocked, windows down. I took a breath and opened a teak veneer door. I was sucked into the Canyon.

A thick soldier in tuxedo pressed my shoulder. It was not a love pat. The soldier was ugly, but I didn't mention it. Both of us were quiet, making up our minds that I wasn't a cop. I wasn't. The tuxedo would have made a good circus tent.

"I hate to ask," the soldier said, "but I suppose you got a name."

"Mitch Roberts," I answered. I had no problem being respectful. "I'm here to see Mr. Canard about a job."

"You don't say," he said. The soldier sported a black wart on his left ear. A nice spray of hair blurted from the wart. He had wide black eyes, black shadows under the rims, and a brown, splotchy complexion. I couldn't see around his shoulders.

"Mr. Reynard sent me over," I said finally.

"You don't say," he spat.

"You'd be good at Scrabble," I said. The soldier pursed

his eyes into slits, swiveled, and strode across the dance floor. I surveyed the Canyon.

I was in an alcove that featured potted palms. They usually do. Through the half-moon doorway, a bored hatcheck girl supported her elbows and a dramatic yawn. She was blonde with black roots. You could have paved Route 66 with her makeup. She had a Jean Harlow glint, but none of the pizzazz. She clicked her gum. She studied her fingernails. The paint job was chipped.

A bloodred carpet snaked into a big room. The room was low-ceilinged and dark. In one corner a horseshoe bar bumped into the dance floor. The bar was black wood and polished glass. There was a blond man in a white jacket behind the bar. Metal stools with velvet seats studded the horseshoe. At one spot, a man and someone else's wife huddled in forbidden jokery. The blond man loomed at the apex of the horseshoe, his hands flat on the wood. He peered straight ahead, a line you could have hung socks on.

The dance floor was a checkerboard reflecting spackled stars from the off-white ceiling. Round tables covered in white linen waddled around the walls like ducks. Candles flickered on the tables. A few couples danced, a bored waiter with his arms folded stood in one of the empty corner spaces. A red-faced man ate dinner alone. The music roared from a gurgly jukebox. It was a small, glittering jukebox, a brilliant stone lodged at the edge of a bandstand. On the raised stand sat a group of chairs, a piano, and a set of shiny drums. Sunday night—the band must have been home soaking their feet. A brass rail on my right led to another shiny portico and a set of stone stairs descended into a brighter haze.

Glass tinkled. Faint casino sounds drifted from below, from down the stone stairs. Chips and clicks and rolling ivory, barkers and dealers spieling. It was far away and subdued.

I lit a smoke. The hatcheck girl fidgeted with her crossword. She clacked her gum again. Paul Desmond music was on the jukebox. I smelled a steak. I remembered I was hungry. The soldier returned.

"Follow me," he said. I followed.

The soldier could have walked to Mars in two hours. We strode along the carpet and down the stone stairs. At the bottom of the stairs we were in the casino. It was a square well of luminescence, two crap tables horizontal to the wall on my left. One of the tables was covered. At the other, a bored dealer watched a businessman toss dice aimlessly for quarters and dimes. On my right hunched a chuck-a-luck rig and a roulette wheel. In back, four blackjack tables stood in line. Two ran with seven or eight players drooped above drinks and cigarettes.

A redhead played roulette. She was wrapped in enough curves to make Warren Spahn proud. A white ball hissed in a track and clicked still. She giggled and sipped a highball. The soldier stopped at another portico in back of the casino. The portico supported a string of glass beads.

"Through here and up the stairs," he said. "Pound a couple of times." I nodded and went through the beads.

Dark stairs climbed in a narrow hall. It was dark and smelled of garlic and must. A single bulb burned at the head of the stairs, but it didn't do much good. I stood on the landing and pounded. The door was pine and it didn't shatter. I heard a grunt. The door swung open when I pushed.

Canard lay on a black couch. He was covered by a racing form. There was a paunch inside his black slacks. Above the racing form a barrel chest heaved. Above the chest his knockwurst head protruded like a lump. He had moles and a small scar on his chin. Greasy black hair covered big ears. His arms were thick, hairy totems, one bent across his creased forehead. On the floor beside his right hand was a tray with remnants of bread, cheese, and tabouli salad and a glass of beer. He had a cigar in his mouth. It smelled like good fish bait.

He poured his fleshy face into my gaze. His face wore a green pallor pleasant as a dog fight. Black eyes wrestled in the middle of his forehead. At one end of the couch a floor lamp illuminated his bare and callused feet. The office was a shamble of papers, metal baskets, receipt books, and filled ashtrays. Canard's desk was hidden by waves of scrap. A bookcase held black binders and a bottle of whiskey. Beside the desk was an easy chair and a standing ashtray. The place was cramped as an outhouse.

"You're the guy Julie sent over?" Canard asked.

"Yes," I said.

Canard hauled himself to the edge of the couch. He kicked the glass of beer.

"Fuck," he growled. His voice sounded like an overloaded pickup. "I suppose you're the guy from Kansas City. Another one of those."

"You'd be surprised," I said. I said it just for the hell of it. I don't know why.

Canard narrowed his gaze. The green pallor turned chartreuse. The face was broad and oval, fleshy-cheeked, mean as cholera in Calcutta. He was short and probably made up for it with bluster and bad jokes. From the garlic and tabouli, I could tell he was Lebanese. Canard stared at me like I was bonemeal and lime juice. Finally, he shrugged. He stuck his cigar between two fat fingers.

"You ever dealt craps before?"

"I play. Never dealt."

"So, what's your name?"

"Mitch Roberts," I answered.

"You get a hundred bucks a week plus tips. You get dinner once during your shift. Your shift is six to two in the morning. You think you can stay awake?"

"I can stay awake."

"You're on table one with a boy named Tony. He'll

deal for the first couple of weeks. You try stickman. He'll teach you the pitch and the hook. You just learn to spiel and sell all the hard ways on the table. I pay the help on Saturday night. You get Monday off, but hang around tomorrow and learn the ropes from Tony. Don't steal from the joint. I'll break your arms."

Canard shifted his weight. There was a tabouli stain on his white shirt and he was born with five o'clock shadow. Sweat adorned his lip.

"Sunday we shut at midnight. What'd you say your name was?"

"Mitch Roberts," I said.

Canard thought for a moment and came up empty. He swept aside the racing form, wiggled his toes, and stood. He hitched his belt.

"Taylor's the doorman. He doesn't say much. Tony's been around, so take it from him." Canard paused. "You a doper?"

"No."

"Stay away from booze. Big rumdum like you should stay away from the customer's wives. Now blow."

I blew. I went down the stairs and through the glass beads. Tony was a small Syrian in a suit and tie. He was sticking for the bored businessman. Tony's mustache slithered along a lip like some starved gartersnake. I walked past the crap tables, up the stairs, and into the alcove. The hatcheck girl was doing a crossword. Tommy Dorsey had replaced Paul Desmond. I shoved a nickel into the pay phone and dialed.

Spud Christian answered after ten rings. He was an ex-G.I. like me. He struggled against the same wake of gray flannel and insurance policies. He lived in a basement apartment, drank ale, and smoked Camels. His chess was good sober and better drunk. He had helped me on a few cases. I slid him part-time jobs to help with the rough patches of unemployment and girlfriends. There were a lot of rough patches. He was a friend.

He helloed with unsteady legs. We talked for a while and I offered him a Jackson to come to the Canyon. I told him to find a burgundy Hudson and gave him some instructions. I told him to wear a sport coat and act tough. I went back into the casino.

Tony the dealer uncoiled his thirty-weight eyelids and tossed me a meaningless look. His peach-smooth face was the color of an olive. Oily eyes looped into a mandolin-shaped face and fuzzy black hair. He held a long white stick in lean hands. The businessman rolled a seven.

''Well, shit,'' said the businessman.

Tony raked five quarters and pushed a pair of red dice to the edge of the table. The businessman rested his paunch on the table and took the dice.

''Coming out,'' Tony said. His tone was smooth as raw tenderloin and horseradish. ''Get 'em down on the hard ways. Play the field. Any craps.''

The businessman was drunk. He rubbed the dice on his shirtfront, brought the dice to his mouth, and blew. He exhaled and tossed quarters onto the green felt.

''Let's see a boxcar,'' he said.

The quarters fell on Any Craps. Music drifted from the dance floor and mingled with the sound of chips and ivory. Voices droned. Above each gaming table, hooded chandeliers corraled a cozy node of light. A garish cashier booth in one corner was decorated with a painted desert motif. The casino smelled of whiskey and steel.

The dice came up five. The businessman finished his drink and drifted to the roulette wheel. Where the redhead was playing. Her body was inside a red dress. The worms who wove the dress were still inside it, too.

''I'm your new stickman,'' I said to Tony.

Tony placed the stick on the rail. He grabbed a cigarette

from a chip slot and lit it with a gold lighter. He inhaled through his nose.

"You gone to see Gus?" he asked.

"Been and come back. I'm on six to two, off Monday. I work with you. You're supposed to show me the ropes."

"Ever deal before?" Tony said.

"No. I've played."

"Know the rules?"

"I know the rules."

"Ever do any heavy spiel?"

Tony sipped ice water. His blue suit covered a bony frame, wide shoulders with padding. Through the fuzzy hair, there was a shiny dome. The chandelier was reflected in the dome. "I mean," he said, "you know we're selling short here, don't you?"

"You lead, I'll follow."

I went behind the table. Tony handed me the stick. In my wool slacks and tweed coat I stuck out like a whore at communion.

"I'm Mitch Roberts," I said. "Maybe I should buy a blue suit."

"Tony Steven," he said. "You look like an overdone college boy." Tony picked up the dice and tossed them. The dice split on four and four. "What are the odds?" he asked.

"Six to five against," I said.

"You know them all?"

"Two to one on four and ten," I said. "Six to five on six and eight. Three to two on five and nine. Coming out, the house edge is five percent. It averages down to seven percent on the Don't Come, goes as high as sixteen percent in the center."

Tony swept back the red dice. "Pretty good," he said.

I looked at the table. Pass and Don't Pass lines rimmed the green. Field Bets, Hard Ways, and Any Craps were in an outlined yellow box in the center. Big Six and Big Eight squared the corners. There are only two ways to beat the house. The first way is to make smart bets on Pass Lines and take all the odds the house allows, play slow, don't drink, don't flirt with the ladies, and go home early if you win a little. The other way is to never play. I didn't figure a lot of players in the Canyon Club knew the game or cared. I figured most of the players drank, flirted, and went home late. It amounted to a tidy profit for the house from a simple game.

The tough craps player rolls dice understanding the odds on every roll. It isn't that hard. When he's losing, he makes small bets, and when he's winning, he bets the limit with house money. The tough player never chases bets to catch up and never plays drunk, tired, hungover, or angry. He never plays with scared rent money. He knows what he can afford to lose, but he plays to win the bank. Houses don't like tough players because they lose small amounts and win big amounts. But houses don't face that many tough players.

A soft craps player makes the funny bets, hard ways, field bets, and any craps, bets that pay off far below the true odds, bets that look pretty and stink inside. When he's losing, the soft player chases his money trying to catch up, and when he's winning, he decreases his bets thinking his luck can't last. He drinks and smokes and pays no attention. He walks into a casino planning to lose a certain amount and always loses it. He is never prepared to win big and loses what he can't afford. He loses the rent money, the gas money, the baby money; he loses his shirt. He blames everyone but himself. Craps is a lot like life in that way.

There is a saying: "In the long run, the house will grind you down." The saying is true except for the tough player. The players in the Canyon probably weren't that tough.

Tony said, "The stickman steers cowboys to the center of the deck. That's your job. Rake the dice and hawk the bad bets. I pay attention to the players and payoffs. All you do for a couple of weeks is make the spiel and rake the dice. I make all the calls and settle the gripes. Nobody causes trouble here. The big guy on the door is Taylor. He's the bouncer. Tough guy, too."

The payoff in the center was twenty percent less than the cost of the bet. Anyone playing the field, hard ways, and any craps has bought himself a ticket to oblivion but fast. My job was to stick and talk up the center bets. It wouldn't be hard to do.

"There're not a lot of numbers players here," said Tony. "Some guys start out playing numbers. They drink for an hour and they can't follow. They end up switching to field and hard ways. There ain't a lot of payoffs when it gets down to it."

The tough craps player allows the dice to run numbers, follows the numbers, and backs his bets by buying correct odds "behind" each bet. The "behind" bet is even money, the best bet any gambler could find, and you only find it in dice games. I didn't think one player in ten even knew it existed. The odds bet is like a kiss from a beautiful girl, but the players never find it. Maybe if they did, the game would change.

"Pass the dice to the right around the table," Tony said. "Treat the ladies nice. They love it and they don't know shit about the game. The drunks out here think ladies are lucky. Let them think it."

He tugged his tie. The redhead and the businessman were side by side at the roulette wheel.

"Canard okay to work for?" I asked.

"Do the work, pal," he said.

Tony tossed dice. I practiced the stick handle, back and forth with different odds and bets. Tony sipped ice water. In ten minutes no one played craps. Time passed. Tony showed me how to cup dice.

"Look out for this one," he said.

He placed the dice in his right hand, one and one on the top. He pinched his hand and sent the dice tumbling in a uniform roll. The dice stopped short of the back wall and fell out snake eyes.

"Snake eyes. Boxcars," he said. "You see some guy cupping the dice when I'm not looking, you let me know. We let Taylor handle those guys."

Dice cuppers pinch the dice with the ones up and roll the dice uniformly along the table, letting the natural forward tumble bring back the ones or their companion boxcars. Guys in back alleys and street corners use it all the time because they don't have a back wall. When the dice hit a back wall, it breaks the tumble and ruins the cup. Casino tables have a back wall and the player is supposed to hit it. Sometimes a player will try to get away with cupping and missing the back wall. It's always "no dice" when it happens. They still try it.

"We get a loader or two," Tony said. "They'll try to slip in one load. It doesn't happen often, but you can usually pick it up because the dice will flop, roll unevenly." I'd seen loaded dice in the army. I didn't figure such dice were common in a tough joint like the Canyon. You'd have to be desperate to try a stunt like that with a gorilla like Taylor on the door.

An older couple approached the table. They played for fifteen minutes and dropped ten bucks on the field. They didn't gulp. The businessman returned and dropped twenty. He was hitting hard ways and any craps. He muttered and left. From the dance floor came the swishy sound of dancers dragging themselves through dust. Taylor stood still, arms akimbo. The redhead played roulette with worms inside her dress.

"Anybody ever try to pick up bets on the house?" I asked Tony. Some players at a crap table will try to grab off other players' bets or rake in losers before the dealer has a chance to check the table. It is the lowest form of cheating but the hardest to break.

"Drunks," he said. "Nothing serious. It wouldn't pay to get caught cheating the Canyon. They cheat themselves just stepping up to the rail."

"What do you mean?"

"You know," he said. "Hard ways, any craps. They might as well tear up dollar bills and eat them. Anybody on the pass line we just have to wear them down." I began to like Tony. He had a nice, warm voice and soft eyes.

"You watch these guys," he said. "They look at that field bet and their eyes pop. Two, three, four, nine, ten, eleven, and twelve. Double on two and twelve. Guy comes off in his pants when he sees the bet. It's a sucker bet. The gaudier the bet, the cheaper the payoff. Remember that." Tony sipped his water.

At eleven o'clock the redhead moved. She uncurled her too-white legs and hopped off the stool. Her moves would have disabled Charles Atlas. The roulette croupier pushed her a stack of chips. She gobbled them, stuck them in her purse, and lit a cigarette. She laughed with the business-man, then flowed to the cashier and cashed in. I excused myself from Tony's patter and followed the redhead. She went up the stairs and into the dance hall. I followed her along the brass rail and into the alcove. Feverish Kenton rolled in the big room. The blond barman hadn't moved a muscle.

The redhead's dress was a flimsy thing, fingerpaint magenta. For my taste, there wasn't enough hip or leg. The overall effect was congenial if you didn't mind standing in line. I get bored standing in line. She talked to Taylor, then passed me and went out the teak veneer doors.

I smoked in the alcove. The redhead had a nice face, mostly punctuation and very little sentence. Her eyes were thyroid brown, dainty cheeks with dimples, red lips done too sloppy for class. The nose was cute, the chin was cute, and the shoulders were cute. Cute walked out my door the first time I saw Ava Gardner in a movie. The redhead's forehead swept into a flurry of auburn gauze that was probably fashionable. A constellation of brown freckles slid into her bodice. She wasn't a floosy, but if she tried any harder she could be. The face was too young to excite my passion. My passion needed muscatel and an amber moon. I stuffed my smoke into a bucket of sand behind a palm and followed the redhead outside.

Spring stars clung to the sky. A strong wind stirred the oaks and hackberries. The redhead flowed along a river of cigarette smoke and diaphanous pink. The pink came from the lights under the peonies. Peonies perfumed the air.

Spud Christian lurked beside the burgundy Hudson. He held his lank form in a hammer and sickle. The redhead flowed past Spud. He grabbed her purse. She hissed like a cat and staggered back. She had her back to a big honeysuckle, a look of surprise rising on her. Spud advanced. I angled for the Hudson.

"What's the problem, pal," I said to Spud's neck.

He turned. "Don't get tough," he said. "Just toddle along and fish yourself some pablum."

The redhead jerked her purse. A compact came loose and she stooped to pick it up. A reasonable flash of bosom appeared. In the moonglow the redhead was all strawberries and cheesecake. Heavy on the cheesecake.

I googooed the redhead. "Is there a problem, lady?" I asked.

"This goon made a pass for my purse," she said.

Spud steadied himself. He wore a leather sport coat, jeans, and a ball cap. He had bottle glasses and a big Adam's apple. He looked like a Dead End Kid.

I curled a short right into his stomach. I pulled the punch. We snorted in unison and Spud went to one knee. He huffed and puffed.

"You've got a choice," I said.

Spud glared up. There was a smile inside the glare. He winked. He rose in an attitude of tense expectation. He pretended to gnaw for air.

"Beat it, or I pawn your nuts," I said.

Spud reeled for a while. Then he adjusted his ball cap and walked quickly to his Nash. It was parked in shadow. He started the Nash and drove down the hill. I fired a Lucky and stood in the wind. The redhead pulled herself together. She took out her own smoke. I lit her cigarette.

"Me Jane," she said.

"Mitch Roberts," I said. The redhead threw her hair into the wind. It flowed north.

"I should thank you," she said. "Thanks. How does it happen you're in the parking lot when I need you?"

"I just took the stickman job. Stepped out to have some air. Kind of slow on Sunday night."

"Mitch Roberts. Sounds familiar."

"We've never met. We still haven't." Her dress was some kind of wraparound silk.

"Agnes," she murmured. "Agnes Reynard. You throw a fair right."

"I specialize in sucker punches."

Agnes smiled. "I like a man who specializes. Everything is so ordinary."

She dragged on her cigarette. Her voice oozed a calm and confident insouciance as if she had experience dealing with undereducated stiffs. She was probably used to guys making quick passes under the influence. After a while, she explored her hip with long, pale fingers. Her nails were long and pointy. Behind us, the businessman staggered to his car and started the engine. Spirea and honeysuckle swirled in the exhaust fumes. Agnes Reynard brushed her hair back. She pinched a tick of tobacco from her lip.

"My husband owns the club," she said.

"I know. He hired me."

Agnes Reynard strolled around the Hudson and got inside. An owl hooted on the hillside. She started the engine.

I walked to the window and stood, smoking.

"See you around," she whispered. It was a sulky whisper, soothing as a glass of codeine.

"It looks that way," I answered. She pushed the Hudson into gear. We looked at each other for a long time.

"Don't worry, muscles," she said. "I don't fuck the help." Then the mockingbird flew away.

SEVEN

Spud Christian sagged on the oak portico. It separated the narrow kitchen from an airy sitting room and dining alcove. His left arm drooped in a circle against his body and the door frame. A cold bottle of cheap ale dangled from the crook of his elbow. With his right hand Spud traced lines on the lead interstices of stained glass imbedded in the supporting wall. He sipped ale. The ale dropped down his narrow throat and passed a bulbous Adam's apple.

He smacked his chapped lips. There was a dreamy, tired glaze on Spud's face. Behind the weary grimace was a hint of resignation and fun. He was slightly drunk, hardly enough to make a difference. He traced the lead interstices and watched me fry some bologna.

Outside, the night moved like a mysterious black frock in the elms. Faint caw reverberations hinted that crows were pushing south and east against the wind, seeking lush corn and wheat in a brotherhood of thievery. Two bongs escaped from old Friend's Clock Tower. Four hunks of sliced bologna sizzled and popped in the iron skillet I held above the gas flame. With my free hand I spread mustard and Grandma's picklelilly on two slices of white bread. Gnats of fat leaped from the skillet, staining the stove. I had worked the crap tables until midnight and returned home to find Spud waiting on the front porch with a bottle of ale. I turned the bologna and lit a cigarette.

Spud cinched his lank form. "There are a few things you don't know about women," he said.

"Do tell," I replied.

"Like, for example, I seriously doubt this fight you staged in the parking lot is going to impress the slinky very much. I could be wrong, but she looks tougher than a plug of Red Man. Spending twenty dollars to knock me in the dust will get you a smile and a handshake. It sure as hell won't get you clean sheets and some dinky-doo."

Spud grinned and sucked ale.

"Well, you're going to find out, anyway," I said. I flipped the fried bologna onto a towel. The towel sucked fat into gray lumps.

"So, spill it," said Spud. He winked wryly. He snagged a Camel from his leather jacket. He lit the smoke, and we stood and walked our sandwiches to the alcove. We sat and ate fried bologna and sucked ale above a chessboard. The tobacco smells collided with the frothy smell of ale and night energy. Spud doused the Camel and concentrated on the food and drink. He studied the chess game. It was an Alekhine's defense, wiry and tenacious.

"I work for the owner of the casino," I said. "Someone is skimming from the till. Someone is also pounding his wife. The guy is blind."

"That's goddamn tough," Spud said. "On both accounts."

"That's what I thought. The owner is a guy named Jules Reynard. He seems like a jake guy. I don't care to work for gangsters, but if someone is skimming, then I can do the work without hitting my conscience with a hatchet. Besides, I felt for him. He lives in the country in a big house. His wife is the little number in red. She stays in town most of the time while Reynard sits in the big house watching red circles on the inside of his head. It is not a pretty picture.''

We ate bologna. I moved a knight. I had a plan for Spud, so I didn't mind telling the story straight. We'd been friends and I knew he could be trusted with anything of mine. Once, Spud had stood up to a knife in a punk's hand for me and hadn't asked any questions afterwards. When I had the time and the money, I'd hire Spud to do legwork. He had the legs and I had the work. Spud captured the knight.

''I figure the skimming is happening in one of two ways. Either someone inside is dickering the books, shorting Reynard on paper, or the cash disappears on the tables to cheating. If someone is tampering with the books, it must be with the knowledge of the manager, a guy named Canard. If someone is cheating the tables, the rainbow gets bright. Either way, it's an inside job. I think Reynard knows that much and that's why he hired me.''

Spud belched bologna. ''What do you mean?'' he asked.

A slab of bologna squirted to the floor from Spud's sandwich. He leaned down to the slab and popped it into his mouth. He moved his own knight and forked a helpless rook on the seventh rank. The rook muttered something under his breath about my incompetence. I'd heard the same complaint before from women and children. I shook it off.

I studied the position and drank ale. I hobbled to the kitchen and poured a tumbler of muscatel. I opened a jar of pickled eggs.

''Last month someone tried to poison Reynard. Or at least tried to put him in the hospital, which they did. While he was in, someone slit some throats of horses he owned. The someone has something to gain from Reynard's business and that could only be someone close to him. He hired me because I'm an outsider and he can't trust his own people. He paid me, and I paid you a Jackson so I could look good meeting his wife. So I could make an impression.''

''So,'' said Spud. ''The red slinky is really Reynard's wife?''

''You got it,'' I said.

Francis the cat slid through a slit in the front screen. He advanced to Spud's shoes and licked fat and grease from the floor where the bologna had plopped.

''I wondered,'' said Spud. ''It wasn't like you to hang around the Canyon. You're a snooker and skittles man, and you like drinking alone. Unsociable and gnarled. How are you going to make progress on the books?''

''Only one way,'' I said. ''I've got to get a look at the books before they're delivered to Reynard. If I can do that, I can tell if the figures are doctored down. A simple matter of paper embezzlement.''

''Those guys are tough. They could pinch your balls.''

Spud was right about that. A man treasured his car, his freedom, his tool kit, and his balls. It was wise to draw the line after losing your tools and your car. I looked at Spud and put down the muscatel. He caught my gaze and stopped chewing.

''Mr. Grant wants your company for two days,'' I said.

''Mr. Grant? For Christ sake, who do I have to kill?''

''Supply me with that camera you borrowed on the divorce job last year. Have the guy ready to develop pictures whenever I need him. I'll give you two Grants, one for you and one for the photographer. I need the camera as soon as possible.''

Spud nodded. ''I can do that,'' he said.

''Then I want you to visit a veterinarian in Augusta. He's a guy named Glick. He must have an office somewhere over there. Reynard's horses were killed in April. Find out where he disposed of the remains, get any photos he took and copies of reports or records he made, quiz him on any opinions he may have formed.''

''I take it the police weren't called?''

"The police weren't called. These guys handle their own problems," I said.

I moved the hapless rook. Spud hopped a knight and captured the other rook. He waved good-bye. My king and queen simpered, sulked, and wrote me a nasty letter. Spud devoured an egg, then another. He wiped an arm across the gooey remains on his lip. I ate an egg and resigned the game.

We rose and I walked Spud to the front screen. A scented night drifted in the doorway. Under a canopy of star and cloud, the sleeping city wheezed.

"Another thing," I said. "See if you can pick up anything about Reynard when he operated out of Kansas City. Tidbits or doodles, it's all helpful."

"Be the hell careful," Spud said.

I peeled two fifties from a roll. I handed them to Spud. After a thoughtful pause, he folded them into his shirt.

"Just be the hell careful," he said. "Guys like you and me we come back from the war without a scratch on the outside and the first Sunday we fall down a manhole after church."

Spud walked to his old Nash and drove south on Sycamore, disappearing gracefully in a forest of Victorian wrecks and storefronts. I stripped and entered the crawlspace of my bed amid rafters of sleep and attic struts of dementia.

I woke from whatever-you'd-call-it. Francis the cat sat practicing scales on my chest. Millions of postmen and plumbers banged around the block, talking to housewives. I showered, ate some toast, and read about Mantle's afternoon in New York. For an hour, I wrestled with the idea of buying a blue suit and a white shirt. I found the suit at the Salvation Army downtown and parted with a ten-spot. I shot some snooker and then pointed the Fairlane toward Black Fox Ranch.

The highway wound through quarter-horse country,

wheat fields, and rangeland. Hills rolled to meet a cobalt sky dotted white with fuzzy cumulus wads. Cala lilies waved in the wet creek bottoms. Yellow sun streamed through the delicate redbud trees; herds of black Angus strolled in grass alive with bees. I wheeled into the gravel drive.

Something was out of phase. I slowed and flipped my Lucky into the roadside ditch. Two cars were parked in the pines, a blue Plymouth and a larger, dun-colored Mercury. I parked beside the Plymouth and walked to the big doors and pounded. Something inside me looked forward to seeing Reynard and to playing our chess game. He seemed like a regular guy, and I appreciated his trouble. The door swung open.

Reynard wore a pale pink dress shirt, deep blue wool slacks, and a white sweater draped loosely around his waist. Black hair swept back cleanly, and he smelled of soap and leather. Tiresias heeled beside him, thirty thousand white teeth glittering.

"It's Mitch Roberts," I said.

Behind Reynard, other figures moved in the big room, one big lump in the recessed area, another smoking a cigarette, his body draped against the wicker bar. Reynard went stiff as an Eskimo Pie.

"Let me handle this," he said quietly. We walked into the big room.

The lump was a size-seventeen neck dressed like a cop. He wore a felt hat inside the house and his brown shoes didn't match his black suit. He was holding a spiral notebook. The middle of his blocky face held a nose that had been broken, reset, broken, and reset.

"Gentlemen," Reynard said. "This is one of my men."

He nodded in my direction. I slid to the bannister that led upstairs and leaned against it, looking bored and annoyed by the delay.

"We'll be through here in a minute," Reynard said in

my direction. I said nothing. The wind and sun entered the big room and emptied into a cloying silence. The cop by the bar snorted.

The blockhead spoke. "You were here all Saturday," he said.

"I don't go out often," Reynard said. "Certainly not Saturday night without any help."

"This Colby," said the cop. "Where is he right now?"

"In town for groceries, fuel, and feed."

The cop made some notes. "I suppose we can have access to him?"

Reynard nodded.

The front door swung open. A small towheaded ferret slid into the room and held his palms open and down. "Nothing doing," he said. He stood there in the open doorway.

"Close the damn door," said Blockhead.

The small cop shoved the door. He grimaced as the wind sucked it into a loud bang. Blockhead mounted the stairs and stood by Reynard. They whispered. Blockhead gestured to his buddy beside the bar. They huddled and whispered some more while the small cop twiddled his thumbs. I noticed Creon poised noiselessly on the outside flagstones. The lake dozed in a limpid atmosphere. I didn't know these cops and I knew my share. The meeting broke.

"We've got to have someone," Blockhead said. "I'm telling you."

Reynard tugged Tiresias alive. He led the cops to the big door and they left. We stood quietly as the two cars roared downhill. I watched the cars curl around the lake and wade into wheat and bluestem. They were gone, finally.

Reynard unfastened Tiresias's leash. He wound it in his hands and wadded the leather cord into the pocket of the white sweater. He descended the carpeted stairs and sat on a zebra couch. Creon slinked through one of the glass doors, made his way across the carpet, and sat erect beside Tiresias.

"Make me a whiskey?" Reynard said.

I walked behind the bar and mixed a Bushmills and water. I coughed when I got to the couch and Reynard took the drink.

"Who are those guys?" I asked.

"Vice cops. Tenderhearted fellows, too. The big guy with the notebook was Dunce Murphy. Only he doesn't like the name Dunce."

I didn't know Murphy. Since Andy Lanham had left Vice, I'd steered away from vice cops. Reynard leaned into the chessboard and moved a knight pawn two spaces. His action surprised me. I studied the move.

"My guess is you've heard about Charlie Allison," I said.

Reynard sipped the Bushmills. I shoved a bishop. Reynard felt the move and smiled. We exchanged a few moves in silence, air and shadow playing in the windows. Reynard lit a black cigar.

"I make payoffs to those guys," he said. "It comes as no surprise they'd be interested in the murder of a reform investigator. Seems Allison was murdered and dumped into the Little River. It happened Sunday morning. Anyone would think I had something to do with it because Allison works for the Democratic candidate. He was making inquiries at the Canyon, probably gathering dirt on my operation to use in the next campaign. Hell, it happens every four years. The outside party always runs to clean up the liquor and the gambling. It would be nice to think that they can be beaten in the election. Right now the D.A. and the governor need to tag someone for this murder. If they don't tag someone soon, then Allison is a martyr. Hell of a ticket."

"May I have a drink?" I asked.

"Sorry," Reynard said. "Help yourself."

Reynard studied the board with his hands, moving them slowly, carefully over the pieces. While I mixed a brandy and ginger ale, he questioned me about the positions. He jumped a knight into the center. I captured a pawn and Reynard moved a rook. He relaxed.

"They've offered to tag you?" I asked.

"Gently so, but yes. The guys in Vice want their payments to continue, but they can't let the Allison case go unsolved. It seems Allison was beaten unconscious by goons and dumped off the bridge. Naturally, I'd be stupid enough to murder him or hire it done. Murphy wants a suspect in a week or so. If I don't give them one, they turn the heat up under me. They apologized and left."

Reynard snapped his fingers. Creon and Tiresias rose simultaneously and trotted through a side door that led to the back of the ranch house. I stubbed my smoke in a crystal ashtray and ascended the carpeted stairs. I stared at the big lake and the hillside that swelled into prairie grass and a fat sun. Reynard sat still, his hands on his blue slacks, his eyes void.

Finally he said, "How did it go at the Canyon last night?"

"Fine. I'm officially the stickman. In fact, I'm on duty in about an hour."

"All right. What about Allison?"

I skirted the sunken area and stood beneath the Klee. On a gray matte field, stick figures balanced geometric items, pink fluff and lyric nonsense. The philodendron was green, the carpet white. I felt dark inside.

"I watched Canard, Colby, and Bunch bounce Allison off the hood of a Buick Saturday night. He was out cold and they drove him away. He wasn't dead then. I know he wasn't dead."

"That's fine," Reynard snapped. "I don't mind them bouncing the clown around, but who killed him?"

"I don't know," I said. Misgivings danced in my conscience. I sipped the brandy slowly. It wouldn't do to show up at the Canyon wearing a buzz.

Reynard stood and stretched. He shrugged, untied the white sweater, and draped it around his shoulders.

"I knew the reform candidate would snoop around the club. It's nothing new, happens every four years. Every time around there's a reform candidate, and when he gets elected, things quiet down and the reform candidate goes on the take. It's a joke. But the snooper is not supposed to get killed. That is not part of the game."

"I don't suppose it was."

"Did you meet Agnes?" Reynard said offhandedly.

"Yes," I answered.

"How did it happen you saw Allison bounced?"

"I was in the parking lot having a smoke. Fly-on-the-wall sort of thing."

I decided to omit the tale of Maple Grove. Reynard had paid me ten thousand to break the skimming routine and to follow his wife. I liked Reynard but didn't fully trust his motives or reactions. It seemed best to keep the secret. It would do no one any good to spill it right now.

Reynard inhaled cigar smoke.

"You realize, don't you," he said, "that this fits in with the poison, the horses, and the skimming?" He pushed his face into an oval of sun. "In a couple of weeks I'll be out of business, sitting downtown in a cold cell. These fools in Vice can't think of any other solution." Reynard drained the Bushmills. "Ten years ago these guys weren't fit to lick my boots." The anger subsided.

"Your position on the board is interesting, I think," Reynard said.

"It stinks," I said. "I've got to go to work."

Reynard ascended the stairs, his movements without Tiresias stuttered.

"What did you think of Agnes?" he said.

"I don't think about her." It was not convincing.

"Very diplomatic." Reynard walked me to the big door. "She was a receptionist with the last expert who attended me. She was the last woman I ever saw clearly. The last woman I'll ever see. It was easy to be astonished under those conditions. Think about it."

"Will you be all right for now?" I asked.

"Hell, yes. But I don't have much time."

I walked to the Fairlane. I watched Reynard standing alone, wind stirring the pink shirt, and behind him the big room open and shining. Reynard's eyes were fixed on a point far away, beyond the grazing horses and Angus, beyond the broad prairie choked by bluestem and wildflowers. I drove down the gravel driveway toward the city and the Canyon, thoughtful.

There were only a few cars in the Canyon lot. A red sun sank behind oaks and hackberrys, long shadows dragged through sand. Traffic swept along Hillside: aircraft workers, soldiers, and salesmen heading home to the wife and kids, a dose of television, and a game of pitch. Inside my blue suit I felt like a loaf of bread. The lapels were an inch too wide, the sleeves an inch too long, the neck an inch too big. Other than that, it fit fine. The shoulders were borrowed from Knute Rockne. No one could complain about the scuffed shoes. I planned to hide them under a crap table.

The Canyon was hushed. The hatcheck girl slid me a come-hither smile oozing rancid honey. Her name was Micki "with an i." She had two little girls at home. The ex came by every two weeks and beat her up once in a while for fun. I winked at Micki and walked to the bar. I ordered ginger ale and drank it.

The dance floor was empty. One of the waiters sat studying his books, counting change. The juke was dead. At the end of the bar, an Air Force tech sergeant nursed a beer. It was five-thirty and in the dusty sunlight the Canyon looked slightly shabby. In the casino, ice and small change tinkled. A slot clanged once. The blond bartender didn't speak. He stood rooted by his hands to the shiny bar.

I thought about Jules Reynard. Following my talk with Maye, I'd followed Bunch and the Syrian to Maple Grove. They had hogtied Allison to the slab. A few minutes later, someone had aimed a busy bullet at my body. The same guy who'd taken the shot had sailed Allison into the river. It was all a deadly setup: the poison, the horses, the murder. I needed to look at the books and I knew my time was limited by vice cops. It made an ironic, brutal sense.

The ten thousand was more money than I ever hoped to have in one place, a chance to head for Montana and buy land, to fish, plant vegetables, grow apples and cherries in the valley of the Bitterroot. A vague awareness rattled inside my skull. Any action impelled by money was likely to subvert rectitude and honor, to make a man lose his senses. I kept telling myself that Reynard was playing it square and that this job was just another case of employee theft, a cheating wife. I'd heard it before. I sipped the ginger ale. The explanation slipped like a ghost into the closet of my heart.

At six o'clock I ambled to table one. Tony the dealer leaned against the back wall, a bored expression impaled on his olive face. No one played craps. There were only a few blackjack customers. The cashier, a small mouse with gray hair and mustache, paced in his booth.

"Bueños tardes, kimo sabe," Tony said.

"Kind of a mixed metaphor," I replied.

"Where the hell did you dig up that suit?"

"I made it myself."

"I believe it," he said.

Tony poured dice onto the green felt. "You'll see why Canard gave you Monday off. It will be slow all night."

In one hour three players strolled to the table and lost money. I sticked and called the hard ways and any craps. It was underwater craps, played in slow motion, silently as guppies in an aquarium. The blackjack tables had more action. Taylor the doorman strode through the casino and disappeared up the back stairs. I didn't spot Canard until eight o'clock.

He waddled through the glass beads and approached the tables. He spoke to a croupier, then stopped beside the crap layout.

"How's he working out?" he asked Tony.

"Swell," Tony said.

Canard eyed me. He wore a blue blazer open over a white shirt, gray slacks, shoes with black tassels. They were rich clothes, but dirty and wrinkled. He smelled of garlic.

"Take a break, Roberts," he said. He looked at Tony. "Close the table. I want to talk with you."

I walked away and watched as Tony covered the felt with blue quilting. Canard walked Tony to the back stairs and they disappeared into darkness. I wandered to the dance floor and pushed open the swinging kitchen doors. There was a rush of steam, fried grease, and garlic. The kitchen looked like a Syrian cruise ship bound for Alexandria. Maye stood in one bright corner beside a cookstove. She chopped scallions. I walked over and touched her shoulder.

She turned and her eyes widened.

"What are you doing back here, Mr. Roberts?" she asked. She was wearing a white smock. Her face glistened.

"I took a stickman job here. Keep it to yourself about us." I put my finger over my lips. Maye said nothing. She turned and resumed her chopping.

"This sure isn't turning out right," she said.

"I'm on break. How about dinner?"

"Rule is," Maye said, "you all eat in the kitchen when we got a crowd. Otherwise, I can serve you at one of the corner tables. We got fried shrimp and garlic salad. That will have to do."

I walked to the bar and ordered beer. I went into the

corner beside the bandstand, sat down at one of the round tables, and lit a smoke. A few couples walzed to Rosemary Clooney. Some bored cowboys rode the bar. The waiters weren't quite busy. I smoked and wondered what Canard and Tony were discussing. I hoped it wasn't me.

I waited. Finally, Maye slid along a back wall of the dance floor carrying a tray of shrimp, french fries, and salad. She placed the tray on the table and looked at me. She shook her head and walked away.

I ate quickly, savoring the garlic salad. Between bites, I saw Agnes Reynard enter the Canyon. She stood in the palmy portico. This time she had on a pair of jeans, sandals, and a lace blouse with rhinestones. Her shoulders seemed thin, densely freckled. In the frosty light, she looked like a little girl. She hustled to the bar and ordered something that wound up red and full of shaved ice. It was not a Wallace Beery drink.

Agnes sipped her drink. I thought about photographing the books. I needed time to slip into Canard's office. I needed to know Canard's schedule, the kind of car he drove, when he took his breaks. Maye might know the details. So would Tony and Agnes. I decided to try to piece together a picture by talking to all of them. It seemed worth the chance, but my hemline went sweaty at the idea. For ten thousand dollars, it seemed necessary. I finished the drink and walked past the bar. Agnes eyed me. I winked.

"Where did you get that suit?" she said.

I stalled for effect. "Made it myself," I answered. I noticed a smile, but it was far away, like a coal-mine fire.

I sticked for three hours. The hushed casino filled with breathless tension. Blackjack players grazed cards and drinks like sheep; slot players fed nickels to their shiny friends. Agnes slipped between the casino and dance floor like a pendulum. A tough would ask her to dance, she'd flirt, dance, then return to the roulette wheel. Her drink turned out to be gin and grenadine.

At eleven o'clock, Johnny Reynard descended the casino steps. He was a scale model of his father, sleek as a palomino, dark as hazelwood. He wore a salt-and-pepper sport coat fitted smartly above a silk shirt. His eyes sat deeply above burnished bone, his hair rolled in waves from a smooth forehead. Three gold rings adorned his right hand. He smelled of whiskey. Agnes Reynard held him around the waist.

"Coming out," I said.

Three players dropped bad bets onto the felt. A platinum number held the dice. She grinned furtively at a bald dope across the table. She threw six.

"The point is six," I crooned. I raked the dice to the blonde.

Johnny Reynard dropped a five-spot onto Any Craps. My stomach growled at the bet. The blonde threw a nine. I raked two bets and scooped the dice back to the blonde. She giggled and the bald dope strolled around the table and pinched her. Taylor walked down the stairs and stood beside Reynard. Agnes ran her hands through Johnny's hair. I noticed. Reynard swayed and dropped another five-spot onto the Hard Way Eight. It was a short, drunk bet.

The blonde threw a seven. I raked in the bets. Tony clapped a dice cup over the bones and covered them.

"New shooter," he said.

He tossed a pair of red dice to Johnny Reynard. Agnes caught my eye. She ran her hand along Reynard's shirtfront. She fed him some gin. He gulped it greedily.

Reynard covered Any Craps and Hard Way Eight with fives. He rolled a seven and Tony paid him.

"This boy is hot," Reynard said. Agnes left the table and returned with what looked like a whiskey and water. She handed the drink to Johnny. He drained it.

"Down and dirty," Reynard slurred. He dropped fives on Any Craps. A cowboy in the corner followed suit. The bald dope dropped some quarters onto the Big Eight. Reynard whirled the dice to the wall. They tumbled into snake eyes.

The blonde clapped. The table was generally pleased. Tony paid.

"Come to Papa," Reynard said.

I raked the dice to him. His face glowed with booze and excitement. He was smaller than his father, but built from the same sleek model. The blonde edged to Reynard and smiled. A few couples tumbled from the dance floor and gathered to watch the hot shooter.

Reynard stayed that way. He held the dice for twenty minutes, rolling craps, hard-way boxcars, and sevens. He lost the dice to a six, and the table groaned. I figured Reynard to be up about three hundred dollars.

"Get your bets down," I said. "Yes sir, hard ways, any craps, bet the field."

Tony smiled. The platinum number covered a hard way. Tony scooped some dice to her and she threw a nine. Then she crapped.

In the next hour, Reynard held the dice four times. He bet the center of the table, folding bills above Hard Ways and Any Craps. Agnes plyed him with whiskey. He tossed deuces, trays, and boxcars. He stuffed the winnings into his coat pockets. At midnight he drifted to the bar. Agnes drifted along.

"Pretty lucky stiff," Tony said.

"I'll say," I replied.

My shift stayed awake for two more hours. Couples finished dinner and drifted to the tables. They lost money and went home. Nobody was hot, everybody lost. Reynard circulated through a few young women who dealt blackjack, Agnes not far behind. He swayed from the whiskey. I helped Tony brush the table and stack chips. Tony emptied the money box. We covered the table with quilting.

"See you tomorrow," he said. "You did just fine."

I washed my face in the washroom and stepped to the

bar. The dance floor was dark; waiters stacked chairs. A black man mopped the floor. He was big, with a fire-scarred face. The blond barman wiped the bar with a towel. I ordered a double manhattan and sat, drinking in the reflected glow of the jukebox. The manhattan was strong and sour. It matched my mood.

Reynard flirted with the hatcheck girl. He stood with Agnes in the pink alcove, then he opened the teak veneer door and waded into the night. Agnes put on a blue jacket and waded after him.

I smoked two cigarettes. Then I finished the manhattan. Anxiety drew inside me like stitches in a wound. I tipped the barman and left the Canyon, heading for a gingerbread and poison-ivy house in Sleepy Hollow. On the way, the stitches snapped and bad blood seeped like a black river into basalt caverns.

EIGHT

Demonic silence fell in the city like erupted ash. It sagged in the elms and hung in the new mimosas like a cloak. I followed my headlamps along the deserted streets, passing rows of residential houses, clinging to expanses of bluegrass and cedar hedge, empty and dark, to whiskered visions of family life, wives sleeping in curlers, children tucked away.

The way to Sleepy Hollow lay past Uptown and along the sedgy shoulder of College Hill, past silent bars and honky-tonks, nearside drugstores, hardwares, and cinemas, and finally into the shrouded bottoms of creeky hollowland. Sleepy Hollow was sleepy and hollow, a fantastical, curvy panorama of brooks and dales and warrens, tangled in the confines of the city golf course. On Yale I parked in the shadow of a thick spirea.

I lit a cigarette. My smoke hung in a glaze of radio glare, and in the glare Gogi Grant sang "The Wayward Wind," her cool tones rising in the smoke, too. On the eastern horizon, through a tangle of cottonwood and maple, Arcturus spiked itself on a black cloth. Preternatural clouds swung in the trees. In the murky distance, a huge expanse of golf course rose and fell in the darkness. I looked at the Tudor.

It was a handsome, squat house covering a corner lot.

A single story of gray mortar wound in a rough L along two sides of the lot. There were two doughnut-shaped panes in each heavy door and a single row of medieval leaded windows at each corner. Ivy climbed the walls up to a walnut panel nestled beneath a thatch roof. Elms covered the square corners. One chalk walkway snaked around an ornate birdbath and disappeared into a concrete driveway. There was a big, white garage in back and a tangle of spirea, chokecherry, and mulberry. It was the kind of place where the Wolf Man would have built an aviary.

Agnes Reynard's burgundy Hudson was nosed up to the white garage. Behind the Hudson someone had parked an MG-A. It was a convertible, sporty enough for the Prince of Wales. From the leaded line of windows in the Tudor, lamplight seeped and wavered. Through the windows I saw nothing save a few solid shapes, bookshelves, a Boston fern, shimmers that passed for gas flames.

I pulled a flash from the glovebox and stuck it in my pocket. Then I hopped from the Fairlane and hiked to a concrete bridge above a quiet, snaking creek. The creek flowed through the heart of Sleepy Hollow and ultimately wound through the golf course. I poked in the thicket beside the creek until a clearing opened beside the Reynard driveway. I leaned through honeysuckle. I could smell the heat of the MG. From my hidden perch, I shot a ray of light into the MG and followed the ray to the front seat. On the steering column was a registration banded to a plastic envelope. The MG belonged to Johnny Reynard. Fifty or sixty heartbeats later, the ice melted from my veins and I went back to my car.

For an hour I camped in the Fairlane while one radio station after another faded to silence. The night air and summer stars burned around me. I tried not to think about the son and the stepmother, or about the blind man alone in his empty house. My own trouble seemed monumental at times; the dreary dishes in the sink, the empty winter nights with the wind alive in the frosty windows, and the inevitable morose ponderings with chess and muscatel as allies. I had, in my own life, confronted the contradictions of hope and despair, wound and repair, and enough boundless buffoonery to last a lifetime. But blindness was a spider in the soul.

The gaslight flickered and the leaded windows gleamed. No one came or went and the lights stayed on. Finally, full of cold fear, I drove home.

At the Canyon, Johnny Reynard had played the wrong bets. Yet he'd come from the table with seven or eight hundred dollars. Some players could toss dice all winter without luck like that, luck that fell on Johnny Reynard like a monarch butterfly falls on a child sleeping in a garden of petunias, luck like a luscious kiss from a fairy princess. I wanted to believe in Johnny Reynard's luck; I wanted to believe in fairy princesses and curly towheads asleep in flowery fields. But in a world of warts and viruses, there weren't fairy princesses. Children went hungry. And eight hundred dollars didn't drop on people like butterflys in a summer field of hay.

I knew it would take time to decide what I believed about the crap game at the Canyon and skimming from Jules Reynard. But there was no mistake about the MG parked behind a burgundy Hudson. Johnny Reynard had won eight hundred dollars at the Canyon Club. He'd pasted himself to Agnes Reynard and left the club at three o'clock in the morning. A million singing butterflies couldn't tell me that he wasn't still there.

I drove slowly through downtown and then across the river bridge under the hulk of the Broadview Hotel, a brown mantis with winking eyes. Near my old house, a vision of the ballpark loomed with gray outfield walls, towers banked against a starry sky. I had only one thought: a simpler life, an easier way to make a living, digging the dirt, tending animals, watching for forest fires from the spicy confines of a watchtower. There was too much trouble with war and childhood, trouble from love, trouble private detecting. Even if I had ten thousand dollars stashed safely in my steamer trunk at home, nothing could make it easy to tell a blind man that his son had spent the night with his wife. I'd give the ten thousand to make it go away.

I whirled the Fairlane behind the row of old Victorians, rumbled down the alleyway, and parked beside the rabbit hutch. The rabbits nibbled thin air. I checked the newly planted garden and went inside the house.

A round head poked above the broken back of my gray chair. Disparate rays from the brass lamp fell on the head. Some snores escaped from it in easy, ponderous notes, risible in the symmetry of sleep. I opened the refrigerator and poured a glass of muscatel. The head jerked.

"Is that you, Mitch?" a voice said.

"Directly," I answered.

The head bobbed. Andy Lanham, homicide detective, looked around the chair. He wiped sleep from his eyes. A blustery, worn-down expression crowned his look.

"Jimmied the door and came in," he said. "I thought you'd be home early. I don't suppose it's early."

"You want a beer?" I asked.

I stood in the kitchen. The sagging walls smelled of fried bologna and bacon grease. Andy rose and shuffled inside his baggy brown suit, easing himself into the creases that grew on cop clothes. He strode to the kitchen and huddled inside the pale refrigerator light. Wind danced curlicues in the bay windows of the alcove. Thunder moved somewhere. The spring smell of dust and rain swam beneath the windy surface.

"I'm here to find out about Allison," Andy said.

I sipped muscatel. The sweet juice scoured an inch of memory from my mouth. I looked past Andy into the alcove. Lamplight and stars mingled in the remains of a chess game, shiny black and tan Staunton pieces flecked by deep haloes.

I'd expected to meet Andy soon enough somewhere in the cracks between friendship and work. Andy had the same problem. We'd faced the difficulty before on some big cases and both friendship and work had suffered, coiled in the uncertainty of morality and necessity. Andy was a good cop, troubled by his responsibilities. Responsibility troubled me as well. Still, we knew each other well enough to pay close attention. It was the kind of atmosphere in which confusion had a chance. We were good friends who needed a fence.

"So how about the beer?" I asked again.

Andy hunched around me. He reached into the refrigerator for a bottle of Pabst. He uncapped it and drank deeply.

"I had a nice conversation with my chief today," Andy said. "It was about the Allison case. Medical finished the autopsy and Allison is on ice in the basement of the station. You recall I told you he was unconscious when he drowned. That's part of the story."

Andy drank again. He stretched his big frame and shoved red hair from his face. His brown suit hung around him like bear skin.

"Let's go into the other room," I said.

Andy followed me. I sat in the overstuffed chair. Andy pushed his rear onto the windowsill and balanced, staring at me. Wind flounced the elms outside. Elm limbs rattled the eaves. Some muscatel fingered a place deep inside me and rested there like a whipped mongrel. Andy began to speak in slow, unmodulated tones. It was the funereal sound of a somber canon.

"Doc found deep bruises on Allison's forehead. He looked closer and found slivers of metal and paint in the hair and in the folds of some lacerations. You don't get metal and paint slivers from falling down in the mud."

"I thought you said the guy was tossed from the bridge?"

"He was tossed from the bridge. When I talked to you, I assumed he was knocked unconscious by the fall. The way it looks now someone bashed his head against a car."

"You assume?"

"Don't be an ass," Andy said. He stepped from the sill and turned his back. He stared for a long time at the dark form of the ballpark across the street. Elms waved wildly. "The doc analyzed the paint," Andy said. "You'd be surprised how much you can learn from a paint job. Black paint, high quality enamel, the kind they dab on expensive cars. It was new factory paint."

"Go on," I said. Andy wanted this out in one blow. I'd let him blow and then it would be my turn. I hadn't decided yet how to explain the situation to him, my involvement with Reynard, my presence in the parking lot that dark night. I didn't think I'd tell him about the cemetery. I didn't know exactly why, but it was the way I felt.

"Anyway," Andy said. "Allison was unconscious when he hit."

He turned and sat again on the sill. "Another thing," he said. "We don't believe he was banged on the bridge. We think he came from somewhere else."

"How do you figure it?"

"Doc found stains on Allison's clothes. There was a little oil and some grease on his suit. Maybe like someone had hauled him on the floor of a car or in a trunk."

"Why couldn't he have been banged, then shoved over the bridge rail at the same time?"

"Why would someone do that? The fall from the bridge would surely knock him out. He'd be easier to haul if he were unconscious. Like I said, it's only a theory."

"So the doc thinks he was knocked out somewhere besides the bridge, hauled to the bridge, and dumped?"

"That's it."

"I saw Allison get banged," I said.

Andy stared at the floor, then walked slowly to the old kitchen. I stayed in my chair and watched the elms dart in the night wind. I heard Andy pouring muscatel into a tumbler. When he returned, he extracted a new cigar from his bearskin and lit it with a wooden match. He exhaled a puff of smoke. The smoke hovered in a wad and ascended to the ceiling. I leaned to the nightstand and flipped on the radio. Soft music played. Elms creaked as the wind rushed in their embrace.

"Of course," Andy said. "You want to tell me about it?"

I fumbled for my pipe. I put some Latakia in the bowl and spent time lighting the mixture. The Latakia smell was like black earth and peat. As I inhaled, the first raindrops tumbled to the rotting porch and kissed the bay windows. Smoke seeped into the walls; the wind rose and swelled and faded.

"I took a job at the Canyon," I said. "I'm supposed to be finding out who's skimming from Jules Reynard. As a sidelight, I'm looking to find what Agnes Reynard does with her evenings, and who she does it with."

"You're working for Jules Reynard?" Andy asked. The disappointment soaked through like sweat.

"Yes," I said.

"He's bad," Andy said. "I didn't figure you to hire on for the bad guys."

"I made up a reason."

"The reason wouldn't be money?" Andy was right and he knew it. There wasn't much to say that God and Aristotle wouldn't see straight through.

I thought for a while. Finally I said, "I had it all worked out in my conscience. At the time there wasn't any problem helping the guy with his wife. I saw him sitting in his big house all alone and I felt for him. Knowing nothing about him, still I felt for him. It doesn't take much to feel for a guy who's blind and whose life is going sour. I made up a reason for working in the casino, too, telling myself that it was just business and that if someone like me didn't do it, then somebody else would. Everybody gambles and drinks, so I figured that finding out about the skimming was just like any other job. Helping the guy spot an embezzler. I told myself that the Canyon could be a bank, or a gas station for that matter.''

''Suppose I go that far with you,'' Andy said. ''I was a vice cop. I took home eighty-seven bucks a week. Still, there were plenty of times when I looked the other way to keep my job. There's some dirt under everybody's fingernails.''

''You could say that. Anyway, I took the job. Maybe there was nothing good about it then. Maybe not now. But I took Reynard's money and I owe him. Something, I don't quite know what. Loyalty, maybe. I won't kill anyone for the guy and I won't hide his dirty laundry if there is any. For now, I'm playing it straight down the line with Reynard until he shows me different.''

Andy sucked some cigar smoke and finally smiled. ''This is funny,'' he said. ''Now tell me about Allison. He's one guy who doesn't have any theories and doesn't find this much fun.''

I went for more muscatel. Andy followed. I cut some bologna and spread mustard on four slices of bread. Then I handed a sandwich to Andy. He stuck the cigar in his mouth and handled the sandwich.

''I was having a smoke,'' I said. ''The first night at the Canyon I took a break and saw Canard and Bunch come out of the back door with Allison. A guy named Colby came along. Then they took Allison and pounded his head against a black Buick. Allison was out cold. Bunch and a Syrian drove Allison away. They loaded him in the backseat and disappeared.''

''Doc was right,'' Andy said.

"As far as it goes."

"You know," Andy said, "this guy Allison worked for the Democrats in the reform candidacy. He spied on the clubs, collecting dirt to use in the campaign if they had to."

"I heard."

"Well, let me tell you something else."

I waited. Andy walked his sandwich into the big room. The brief rain had stopped, leaving the elms steamy. A morning dove cooed low notes, resonant and looped.

Andy said, "I'm off the case."

I unlaced my shoes. Andy's face paled and he put on his felt hat. He didn't eat the sandwich. It stayed in his hand like a softball.

"What's going on?" I asked.

Andy drained the muscatel from his glass and puffed on the cigar. His face reflected weeks of sleepless activity, his blue eyes rimmed red, lines and creases riveted at the mouth and brow.

"The D.A. took Homicide off the case. The office is working it as a vice case because of the connection to gambling, liquor, and the election. In reality, the boss wants the whole case put on hold for a week. He's trying to let the boys at the state capitol decide what to do. In short, they've got to find a patsy for Allison's murder or the Democratic ticket will ride into office on the corpse. They'll ride the corpse hard and put it away wet."

"How does that mean they take Homicide off the case?"

"Guy named Murphy is head of Vice now. He knows Reynard, Bunch, and the rest of the boys who run gambling and liquor in this town. If Murphy can give the D.A. a suspect with enough clout, then they can take the heat off the election in the newspapers long enough to put the case to sleep. Vice finds a suspect and the payoff scam stays the same. If they can't find a patsy, then the Democrats will play hardball reform and probably win the election. If that happens, then the D.A. is out of a job, and so is the whole vice squad and half the Republicans in town. They need a murder suspect, Mitch, and they need one bad. They need a suspect bad enough to tag Reynard."

"I follow," I said.

"Another thing. Reynard looks real good for it now. They think they can set him up as the guy who hired it done. I know he's blind, but if Vice pinches him, the heat will be off for a while. Even if he's not convicted, the heat will be off, and your boy Reynard can find another career. He'd be through here."

I thought that over. "Unless someone finds the killer," I said.

"You mean Mitch Roberts, boy detective?"

"It might be both of us."

"You forget I'm off the case," Andy replied. Then he frowned and took off his hat. "You've got my interest."

"I told you I watched while Bunch and Canard bounced Allison's head on the Buick?"

"Yeah, so?"

"I followed Bunch and a Syrian when they took Allison for a ride. Allison was alive then."

Andy spoke. "He drowned. So he wasn't dead during the drive."

"Those guys drove Allison to Maple Grove. I hid out and watched while they tied him to a cemetery slab. Bunch and the Syrian drove away in their Buick."

"Do you figure Bunch and the Syrian returned and took him away?"

"I don't know," I said.

"Tell me more," said Andy. "Remember, I'm off the case."

He smiled, put down the sandwich, and took off his suit coat. He threw the coat onto the brass bed, undid his suspenders, and let them drop to his sides. In the kitchen, he retrieved a green gallon jug of muscatel and brought it back to the big room. We filled our tumblers.

Outside, gray strokes painted the east. Pink creases broke above the outfield wall of the ballpark and twitters erupted. Jays and finches yawned. Andy walked to the alcove and slid an oak chair beside my big gray outfit. He twirled the chair and draped himself over the back, his arms dangling on its lattice supports.

"I love this shit," he said.

"I saw Allison on the slab for a few minutes. Then another car pulled into the cemetery and drove straight to Allison. I ran away like a good boy. Whoever was in the car took a shot at me."

"Jesus Christ," Andy said. "He missed?"

"This time," I answered. "I drove away and didn't know anything about Allison until the next day when you told me he'd been found dead."

Andy drank some muscatel. His face flushed pink like the sky. "How do you figure it?" he asked.

"How about Bunch and the Syrian? They could have had a change of mind and come back. Dumped Allison in the river."

"It doesn't make sense that way," Andy said. "Too much wasted motion and time. We apply Newton's principle of parsimony to explain things in the simplest way possible. Why would they run the guy to the cemetery and then come back?"

"Right," I said. "And they didn't have time to get a change of orders from someone else, either."

"So you rule them out?"

"Absolutely. For now." I sipped muscatel. Sparrows wrecked their lungs, cheeping.

"So who do you figure?"

"Anybody else," I said. "In the dark I couldn't recognize the car or the guy. Come to think of it, I don't know that it was a guy. It could have been a woman."

"Give me a hint."

"Well, my first thought was of Colby, guy who works for Reynard. If it was Colby, he could have had the time. It could have been Canard, guy who manages the Canyon for Reynard. Canard knew where Allison was headed. The motive would have been to get Reynard pinched and take over the business."

I turned off the brass lamp. The big room was bathed in a formless light. I surveyed the burnished floor, the olive drab blanket on the bed, oak chairs, and antique oak table. There was fishing gear, books, and cartons of pipe tobacco scattered in counterpoint to dead cacti and my prints of Hopper and Schlecter. The room seemed comfortably tired. It held the faint rain smells of tea roses, mimosa, and honeysuckle. The neighbor's rooster crowed twice and stopped.

"Any other ideas?" asked Andy.

"Agnes Reynard," I said.

"Reynard's wife. Sleek number who sleeps late?"

"You know her?"

"Met her when I worked Vice. She gets around, but then again so does syphilis. What makes you think of her?"

"Just thinking. I still think too much."

"Let's back up," Andy said. He poured another muscatel. I took the jug and poured one myself. Andy's face grew red. He looked medium rare. "Why kill Allison in the first place?"

"What I said before was just guesswork. Really, I don't know. Andy, I found a note pinned to Allison at the cemetery. The note said that if he came around the Canyon again, he'd be underground. Did the cops find the note?"

"No note," Andy responded. "Whoever killed Allison did away with the note. Didn't care about giving him another chance at the Canyon. It would seem to make it one of Reynard's boys, not his wife."

"Could Johnny Reynard have done it?"

"You mean the kid Johnny?"

"Yeah, his son."

"I'd say yes if Jules had told him to do it. Ordinarily, I'd say Johnny Reynard isn't ripe enough to pick for a job like that. He's small-time. Maybe, though, he's stupid enough to try to break into the big time with a scheme like this."

I thought it over. "If Reynard wanted to double-cross his pals, then he could have had his son waiting at the cemetery. Slick as hell, he could have come into Maple Grove and done the job."

"That doesn't work, either," Andy said. "Reynard would have known the finger would point at him."

"Maybe Reynard actually wants to give Vice his son as the patsy. Think about it."

Andy doused his cigar. One junker lumbered up Sycamore and stopped at the corner. Gears clanked. It chugged away.

"What's Reynard's motive in giving Vice his son?"

"All right," I said. "I don't have much. Just a lot of idle theories splashing around a big, black ocean. We need a kiddie pool fast." I was trying on ideas like old suits. Nothing fit unless you knew about Agnes and Johnny. There was a reason for Jules to frame his son.

Andy stood. He weaved the suspenders around his shoulders, dove for his hat, and found it on the bed. Striped sunlight lay on the brass bedstead.

"Shit," he said. "I'm off the case. If you come up with something, give it to me. I'll keep my ears open. This whole case could be connected to the skimming at the Canyon. All I know is, I need a bath." Andy donned his hat.

I followed him to the porch. He leaned against the rotted railing, one hand on the balustrade. Pure cobalt morning poured through the elms.

"What are you going to do?" he asked.

"I'll try to check the books at the Canyon," I said.

"Keep my eye on the tables for skimming. It should say something about why Allison was killed. What, I don't know."

Andy said, "Those guys are all rough. Keep your eyes open." Andy turned and pushed his hulk from the rail. "I guess that didn't come out right, Jules Reynard and all," he said.

A milk truck stopped down the street. The milkman hopped out and towed a rack of milk and cheese to one of the old Victorians. Beside Andy, a green garden spider rested in the vortex of a silk web. Dew rested there as well. Air moved in the web like fingers on violin strings.

"You know," Andy said. "A spider spins a perfect web. Then he eats the damn thing and starts again the next night. Spider is perfect, not like us."

Andy and I stood quietly. The milkman ascended the rickety old stairs and handed me two bottles of milk. He smiled and went away.

"You be careful," Andy said. It was the second time my friends had said the same words to me. I watched Andy drive his blue Plymouth down Sycamore and stop at Maple. Then he drove east across the bridge toward his home, his wife, and his children.

Robins clowned in a peony patch. Early morning chimed a clear, soft note. Half cockeyed, I slept in my blue suit, with neither dream nor movement.

NINE

In the morning, Rita slipped into my consciousness. She wore lizard green. It flowed down her body like a river in pinyon pine country. Xavier Cugat played a one-note samba and the samba shivered in Rita's hair like sunbeams. I rolled over and looked at her.

She had cool mica eyes, articulated bones, and a long, mannered neck. Her skin was the color of a Sandusky peach, fuzz and all. Long fingers and pale hands hinted sensuality and sensitive indifference. It was the kind of question a man always wonders if he can answer. Her legs were shapely as palms on the beach. Rita wet her lips with a red tongue.

I smiled as Rita danced to my side and looked down. She placed her body on the bed and held a soothing conversation with my soul. Then she touched my temples; my own gaze was on the temple of her stomach that rose and fell like an angel wing. It was a flat stomach with the hint of womanly bulge. I heard a samba inside. Rita ran a finger through her hair. It smelled of straw and apples. I reached for her thigh and Rita slipped a tongue into my ear.

I woke as Francis the cat snored purrs into my face. He stretched, yawned, and licked my ear. Francis in the morning sun was the color of a Sandusky peach, fuzz and all. He smelled of backyard straw, not at all of apples. His furry stomach bulged, probably from mice. I rubbed sunlight and sleep from my eyes. Francis meandered across the blankets and yanked his body down off the bed.

I looked at my blue suit. It had all the homespun charm of a two-car crash, all the wrinkles of very old money. I raised myself from bed, took a long shower, and walked the suit up the back stairs to Mrs. Thompson's three rooms. I gave her three dozen eggs and a stack of bananas. Mrs. Thompson ironed the suit. Then I weeded and watered the garden, fed the rabbits, and tried to clean the clutter from my rooms. Then I sat in the alcove and made some calls.

Spud Christian didn't answer. I knew time was short for Jules Reynard, and what I'd seen parked in the driveway at Agnes Reynard's gingerbread house last night didn't make me think that the answers I would provide Jules would make him happy. I was willing to be patient with Johnny and Agnes, but I couldn't afford to let my knowledge cool its heels while Jules cooled in a cell downtown. If Jules was going down for the count, then I wanted him in the ring with his corner men, including me. Misgivings and concerns rambled around my conscience looking for appropriate loopholes and dodges, but nothing could convince me I didn't owe Reynard some loyalty after taking his money. Even Andy Lanham hadn't questioned that judgment. It was one I'd have to live with. I hoped I could. Working for a thug was not my idea of Sunday school.

I gagged on the thought of Johnny and Agnes alone in the house on Sleepy Hollow. Johnny was full of himself, loaded with charm and flair. In most situations, I figured he could be harmless enough, as most charming men are. Agnes was like sulfur matches. You needed to close her cover before striking. I didn't think Johnny had sense enough to close covers anywhere. Agnes looked tough, a dental receptionist with an enamel heart. She was a gold-digger with claws. It seemed likely to me she would try to destroy her husband if she stood to gain. She stood to gain.

I supposed that Johnny stood to gain, too. Everybody stood to gain except Jules, who stood to lose. Just a blind thug whose time had come and gone. The crudity of the situation chilled me.

I put on some dungarees and drove to a game and novelty shop built into the recesses of an old saloon on West Douglas. This part of town had been where Wyatt Earp and his friends held forth, and the streets were old and brick and packed with facades. From the joke store I chose a couple of pairs of red gambling dice and a chapbook on dice: loading, palming, and cheating. At a mom-and-pop on Maple I bought a big T-Bone, tomatoes, lettuce, and a gallon of orange juice. I stocked up on smokes, muscatel, bologna, swiss cheese, and pipe tobacco.

I puttered and broiled the steak, made salad, and drank some orange juice. In early afternoon, I rocked on the front porch and read the chapbook. The steak was juicy, and early spring was everywhere with lilacs, tulips, peonies, and red tea roses. The sky was soft as milkbreath, the air pure blue as Miss Muffet's corset. From the ground there escaped a mushy aroma of roots, tubes, and stems. Robins stuck beaks into black loam and hopped like popping corn.

The sun swept south and east, and Mrs. Thompson joined me on the porch. I fed her some tomatoes, romaine, and lemon iced tea. She nibbled the salad like a rabbit, and we watched the sun dance in elms, showering the yard with warm shadows. I phoned Spud again, but got no answer. I was anxious to get the camera and take a look at the Canyon's books. I knew there should be two sets, one for Jules and another for Canard. Gus Canard had to be in on the skimming, otherwise it was an inside cheat job from the tables. What I'd seen of Johnny had made the second possibility possible.

Mrs. Thompson watched as I used my Staunton chessboard as a table. I put the chessboard on my knees and for an hour practiced palming dice. I scattered four dice on the chessboard at random. Crooking my thumb and index finger, I held an extra die in the hollow space made by two fingers. Then I swept my hand above the four dice on the table, finally settling a palm above one. Pretending to take one of the die with my fingers, I picked it up with my palm and released the hidden die, sending it spinning along the chessboard, at the same time holding the new die in my palm. I practiced fast and slow, sweaty and calm, then practiced with two dice in my palm, tossing a third.

After the first hour, I switched hands and practiced with my left. I discovered I was right-handed with a vengeance. Mrs. Thompson thought I was touched.

The three-thirty factory whistles blew south of town. It was a long groan and a worker's lament, the solid major chord of wage slavery and family life. Mrs. Thompson shuffled away and returned with my blue suit neatly pressed on a wooden hanger. She had added a white handkerchief. On the lapel was a pale red tulip.

I phoned Andy Lanham at the station and left a message, then drove to the office and scouted around. There were three messages slipped under the door. One was from an insurance agent, one was from a typewriter repair shop, and the third was from World Book Encyclopedia. The World Book suggested that each of my children would be dunces without their product. I went into the office and paid some bills and wrote notes to some steady clients explaining the situation. Jake the barber stuck his head around the corner with a hello. We made a fishing and baseball date, then I drove home.

I took a hot bath and sat on the brass bed with orange juice and Rita dreams. The five o'clock news foretold storms from Nebraska, high winds, rain, and hail. There was nothing about Charlie Allison. Mantle had a good day in New York. The Thumper popped two in Chicago. In general it was a fine day for everyone except Charlie Allison and Jules Reynard.

In the flat evening sun, the Canyon appeared like an aged flamingo. Pink paint chips lay scattered in the peony beds. The desert scenes were all faded. There were languid tones in the amber sun and rising dust. I sat in the deserted parking lot and smoked a Lucky and thought of the Canyon as a fat madam, not retired, but on her way out. Too much paint and too many miles. I went inside.

The bottle blonde stiffed me with a frown. I didn't flirt enough to make it worth her while to smile. I went to the bar for my ginger ale. I took the glass into the kitchen. In one corner a Syrian was beating a naked chicken. The chicken didn't fight back. Maye held her feet on a metal stool. She was smoking a small cheroot. Fluorescence smothered the room with woolly glare. Dishwater, grease, and MSG soaked from white walls. Maye stared at me.

"Good evening," she said. There was a look of mild disappointment in her expression.

"Maye," I said. "Do you know what kind of car Canard drives?"

"You just won't quit," she replied.

She sucked her cheroot. An incandescent dot appeared at the tip and a spool of smoke escaped. Behind me, another chicken split with a crack.

"He drives a big Cadillac like you and me never going to own."

"What color?"

"It looks like a gun."

"How about some dinner about seven-thirty?"

"You come back here to the kitchen. We're going to have more customers tonight than last."

"What's on the menu?" I asked.

Maye rolled the cheroot in her hands. They were cracked and burnished as horsehide by linseed oil. From the dance floor marched some dispassionate Harry James, one trumpet and a short stack of trombones.

"I'll have you some veal and peppercorns. There's some

kibbe, too, if you want it. But I don't know what you're doing working for Mr. Reynard, a man like that. I don't do nothing but cook, but I don't know what you're doing. I just look around and see things. You know what I'm saying, Mr. Roberts?"

"Trust me, Maye," I said. "I'm trying to do right."

"I sure hope so," she said. "You're a nice boy."

That's right, I thought. I'm a nice boy. I touched Maye and told her I'd be along at seven-thirty. She nodded and managed a small smile, more hopeful than meant.

Maye looked at my suit. "That tulip does look nice, Mr. Roberts," she said.

I finished the ginger ale and went to table one. Tony leaned drowsily against the back wall.

"The tulip is nice," Tony said.

"I made it myself," I answered.

In my suit pocket, two red dice burned cool holes. I helped brush the table, stack chips, and count money. Those dice grew heavy and complained about lack of oxygen. It started me thinking about religion and justification by faith. My heart raced.

Tuesday evening at the Canyon oozed like gray clay. Shortly past seven o'clock twenty square dancers plunged to the floor in a rondo of hay-nonny-nonnies and dosey-does. The women cantered around the dance floor in white crinoline and lace piled above fifty yards of fluffy slip. All were portly and toothy, raised on fried bacon and rhubarb pie.

Their partners were scrawny bucks wearing black string ties, dark wrinkled trousers, and white cowboy shirts. The square dance droned in the casino like an earache. They wouldn't gamble, but they drank a little whiskey and ate beef.

At the table, a tired factory hand lost five dollars and ambled his body out the door. There was no sign of Agnes or Johnny, or of Colby. The hatcheck girl picked her teeth with a fingernail file. I sticked and talked baseball to Tony. He didn't seem interested in sports, chess, or politics. He wanted a new Mercury and a path to the hatcheck girl's thighs. At last we settled on bored silence.

At seven-thirty I went to the kitchen. I ate veal piccata, garlic salad, some kibbe, and a slab of apple pie with cheese. I drank some mineral water and listened to my liver yodel. My kidneys doffed a hat. Then I went into the parking lot with a cigarette and found Canard's gunmetal Cadillac parked beside the back stairs that wound to his second-story office.

I walked back inside and through the kitchen to survey the back approach. A steep bank rose from the edge of the parking lot into hackberry and oak. Two windows peered bleakly from the office onto the wilderness. The windows were shuttered and grim. Dirty yellow rays escaped the shutters and tinkled on the cutbank like lost pennies. The door at the top looked like plywood and tenpenny nails, a simple Yale lock above a handle. I'd been in Canard's office and hadn't noticed a safe or strongbox, and the office didn't look burglarproof. Perhaps I could jimmy the door, take some pictures, and scamper down the back stairs. It could be done and it had to be tried.

During the next two hours a couple of sump-handle brothers from Haysville lost money. They complained and groaned and breathed fire. They rolled sevens and twos and bet foolishly. A mousy waitress delivered shots of whiskey to the brothers. Three hundred down, they staggered away, openly surmising that the dice were crooked, the table crooked, the stickman crooked, the dealer crooked, and God Himself a miserable NO-GOOD. One lady in mink watched her starchy husband lose thirty dollars. They argued and left. Gus Canard came down his stairs and wandered into the casino. The square dancers went home after dinner.

Johnny came in at eleven-thirty. He handed the hatcheck

girl a new borsalino. She giggled and flirted with stunted eyelashes. Johnny shook Taylor's hand and staggered down the casino stairs. He wore a powder-blue oxford shirt open above a cashmere cardigan sweater. Two stiff legs balanced drunkenly inside his pleated trousers. Johnny smelled of Canoe and whiskey.

Across the room, Canard snapped his fingers. The mousy waitress appeared with a shot of whiskey and handed it to Johnny. He smiled and slugged the whiskey. His gills pumped alcohol and hot carbon. I saw Agnes Reynard amble down the stairs and sit at a roulette table. Canard clapped Johnny on his cashmere back. Agnes crossed her legs inside an orange sun dress. Her knees were bony, not like Rita's at all.

Couples played slots. The casino shimmered from the sound of bells, clangs, gongs, mutterings, comings-and-goings, glass, and ivory. Johnny and Agnes played roulette and seemed to be winning. The blackjack tables hummed. One tall gent in a black tux attracted a crowd with a string of drunken wagers. He lost. The crowd murmured. Winning seemed more exciting to me, but I wasn't a crowd.

Past midnight, Agnes and Johnny walked in a smoky filigree to the crap table. They joined an Air Force captain and an anniversary couple. The captain played right, tough craps, betting numbers, taking the odds. In an hour, he had managed to eke out twenty-five dollars and was satisfied with his showing. The anniversary couple spatted and lost. Johnny leaned above the table, glee on his smooth features. Agnes clung to his waist like an inner tube.

"Coming out," I said.

Tony hopped some red dice to Johnny. He cupped them and gave them to Agnes. She blew on the dice and smiled. Johnny tossed a ten-spot onto Any Craps and rolled a twelve. Tony paid and returned the dice to Johnny. Johnny snapped his fingers for the waitress.

"Fish in a barrel," Johnny said. He stared at my red tulip. "Man here rolls nothing but heaven."

His Canoe evaporated into whiskey and he shoved another ten onto the center bets. He shot the dice, hitting the wall hard to an eleven.

"A winner again," Tony said. Tony slid a pile of chips to Johnny. I sticked the dice to Johnny and Agnes picked up the red cubes and held them to her breasts. With her cheeks flushed rust color, black eyeliner, red lipstick, she was cute as a box of spoiled Red-Hots. She belonged in the lost and found at the bus station.

Johnny held the shoot for fifteen minutes, horsing field bets, any craps, and hard ways. The Air Force captain lost his twenty-five on right bets, grunted, drained his vodka, and went home. The anniversary wife got sick and was carried to the car.

"Some dice," the captain said as he left.

"Some shooter," Tony said.

I waited for a chance. At the end of the night, it came. Johnny left the table for whiskey. When he returned, he stood against the far wall, tossing dice my way. Agnes found his side and they kept shooting wrong dice, craps, field bets, and hard ways. Johnny was up three hundred dollars. Then the dice hit the back wall and rested on a seven.

"A winner," Tony said. He reached for the dice.

I palmed one of the twins in my pocket and scooped the shooters from the table. I hooked a thumb behind one of the pair and slipped the substitute and its mate across the table. Tony halted and glared. He studied the dice and returned them to Johnny. Johnny lost two bets and left the table with Agnes on his arm like a hound. I stuffed the shooter in my pocket. Bill Halley's drummer smashed my heart with a stick.

The casino emptied. The tall gent in black left and his crowd followed. The mousy waitress gathered drink glasses as the croupiers brushed their layouts. I covered the crap table and said good night to Tony. In the main room, waiters stacked chairs and the fire-scarred man swept the floor. Small houselights buried in the spackled ceiling revealed dust, disuse, and food stains. The nameless barman feigned an expression of bored unconcern. Behind the feign was a mask and behind that a mirror. I walked outside.

Night drained through the elms. Peonies and black earth joined the wind. I smoked a Lucky and strolled to the side stairs. There was a gunmetal Cadillac parked at the base of the stairs. The burgundy Hudson and the MG were gone. I tossed the Lucky into a chuckhole and drove toward Sleepy Hollow. The streets were deserted and no one followed me.

I put the shooter into the pocket liner of my suit. Johnny Reynard had used the cube to collect another three hundred of what table one owed him. Either he was blessed as a swaddled babe or the dice were lumpy. I cruised down a dark Central Street and wound into Sleepy Hollow feeling sour as old tennis shoes. I knew what I'd find at the gingerbread house and it wouldn't be Hansel and Gretel.

I drove slowly past the house. The Hudson and the MG were parked in the driveway. I drove away.

Spud's Nash sagged in front of my old Victorian. I rolled into the alley and rumbled into my slot beside the rabbits. Wind rose in the elms and the rabbits twitched nervously. Thunder shook in unknown places. Across the fence, chickens clucked under their breath. I walked to the side of the dark house and mounted the front steps. Spud tossed his Camel and rose.

"How's the stickman?" he asked. Spud wore paint-stained dungarees and a ball cap. His work shirt was misbuttoned.

"Come in. I've been trying to call you."

We went inside the old house. I flipped on the brass floor

lamp and went into the kitchen for orange juice. Spud searched the refrigerator for muscatel and poured a glass.

"What's the story?" I asked.

Spud reached into his back pocket and extracted a small camera. He handed it to me.

"The guy was out of town. That's why it took me two days. I had to call his wife and she let me into the shop. I talked to the guy on the phone and he'll do the developing. The fifty dollars was fine."

I changed clothes and Spud made bologna sandwiches. Then he smoked a Camel on the porch and watched the wind. I pulled the brass lamp into the alcove and turned on the overhead lamp. I dropped the shooter onto the oak table. It shimmered like a ruby.

"What the hell is this?" Spud said. He munched the sandwich.

"Johnny Reynard has been shooting the lights out of table one at the Canyon. He's been doing it with this."

Spud fondled the cube. He held it up into the brass lamp.

"Let's roll some craps," I said.

With the chessboard, I made a wall. Spud clacked the die against the board and it rebounded onto the oak surface. It showed six. He tried again. He threw one, then six, one, one, six, and one again. Spud whistled and threw a lonesome three. In fifteen tries, he tossed six and one twelve times.

"I'd like to own a pair of these," he said.

I rummaged in the kitchen and found a pocketknife. When I returned to the alcove, wind banged the windows. Spud studied the cube.

"You say Johnny Reynard won money with these clangers?"

"Around fifteen hundred in the last few nights."

"You think he's cheating?"

I looked at the cube in the brass halo. I rubbed the knife blade across one side of the die. Red paint chipped away and I sensed a rough spot in one corner. I picked at the spot with the knife point. A chip fell away from the corner.

"What the hell?" Spud said.

"Tungsten," I said. "Commonly used to load dice. This particular beauty probably has half a dozen loads. It obviously comes up one and six. Makes a nice way to roll boxcars, any craps, and hard ways. Snake eyes. For a guy who bets the center of a crap table, it would be money in the bank."

"I see what you mean," Spud said. He thought. "You think Johnny Reynard is stealing from his old man?"

"I think so. But he's getting help from the club manager. It's a slick way to skim club profits until Canard and Johnny can get rid of Jules. Simple and unbeatable."

"How did you get the cube?"

"Palmed it from the table tonight."

Spud finished his sandwich. Francis the cat strolled into the alcove and hopped onto the table. He purred and picked at a cockleburr buried in his neck. I flipped on the old Philco radio and found some Nat Cole. Black bushy clouds rumbled low in the north and west. Spud adjusted his glasses.

"I talked to the veterinarian in Augusta," he said.

"What's the story?"

"He didn't mind talking, but he didn't have much to say. The doc used to work for Reynard at the Black Fox on a regular basis. Seems the ranch ran a pretty-good-size herd until four or five years ago. Since Reynard went blind, they only keep three or four horses around. Your friend Colby feeds the horses and there was a Mexican who cleaned the stalls and hauled alfalfa.

"Doc Glick remembered the Mexican fellow called during the night some months back and said a couple of horses had been killed. Glick drove to the ranch to take a look. He says that he saw Colby and that the horses looked pretty badly torn up. Colby doused the mess with gasoline and set the horses on fire. Glick drove back to town an didn't think much about it. Says Colby told him he should mind his own business. Glick says he knew Reynard was a gambler or had a shady reputation, so he figured it was some kind of vendetta. Glick hasn't been back to the ranch and has no intention of going. Seems Colby let the Mexican go."

"Glick didn't have any records, photos, or notes," I said.

"Didn't need any."

"How old were the horses?"

"Says they weren't even broke yet."

"Thanks, Spud," I said. "I appreciate the information."

Spud stood. "You look tired," he said. "If you're going to use the camera, I hope you've got a way out."

"I've got a plan," I said.

"I'll tell you something else. I talked to some of the guys down at the White Way snooker hall. These guys were old stiffs and gamblers themselves. They'd heard stories about Jules Reynard. There was this one guy named Sammy said he'd heard a story about Reynard when he was still in Kansas City. Seems he heard about Reynard's first wife and how she ran around town with a young hood on Reynard's time. Reynard found out about his wife and the hood. Well, a couple of butchers found the young hood heels-up in a meat locker at the Armour plant. Someone found Reynard's wife, too, only they found her in the Missouri River under a railroad trestle."

Lightning creased the sky. Nacreous slashes appeared like stars in the bay windows. Thunder followed.

"I'm glad to hear it," I said.

Spud walked to the front screen. Francis tagged along, rubbing his back on Spud's leg. Rain whispered in the trees, thin sheets struck the black pavement. It fell in a brief, blue cascade.

"This guy Sammy said the wife was murdered in nineteen thirty-eight. I don't think your Jules Reynard is a simple fellow. Sammy thought he was a hard case."

"Thanks, Spud. I'll consider it."

"See you tomorrow?" asked Spud. I nodded.

Spud sloshed into the rain and drove his Nash into the night.

I stripped and lay down in the dark. The rain stopped and the wind died.

TEN

Humans are weeds converged in furious war. Their perpetual assault exterminates beauty and denies cultivation its due. I began to think of my involvement in the Reynard case as an example of weedy growth masquerading as work. In three days, I'd learned about Jules, Johnny, Agnes, and Gus Canard, and there wasn't a decent trait among the lot. I'd done it for money. There wasn't any excuse about that, and what I needed was a decent, honest way out, a way allowing me to keep some self-respect and a batch of honesty. I hoped the answer was a trip to Black Fox Ranch, a report on skimming, cheating, and a graceful exit, stage left. Weeds are sticky, unlovely things. I felt them growing in my garden.

I entertained these Hobbesian musings while rocking on the front porch in a diminishing patch of sun. I had a quart of orange juice and a volume of end games by Rubenstein before me. At the office I'd chased down a Hudson for the First National Bank, served two subpoenas for my lawyer pal Graybul, and stuffed some ad envelopes. The back garden was watered, the cat fed, the rabbit hutch cleaned. My new blue suit was well-pressed, and I'd picked a fresh tulip for the lapel. Finally, I showered, fluffed my physique, and prepared to leave for the Black Fox.

I sealed Johnny Reynard's die in an envelope, loaded

the small camera, and put the camera in a leather reel bag. I put the reel bag under the front seat of the Fairlane. As I drove across the fields to the Black Fox, I used the time to think. Late afternoon ambled on the prairie, cloud shadow and hushed willow playing on bluestem. Horses gamboled, paints and Arabians and good quarter stock. Angus cattle grazed dumbly on green hillsides. The sun poised amid white cloud, lazy creeks rippled, and the wind stirred clumps of delicate redbud. It was the kind of day to lie down on a blanket with Rita and run your hands along her flanks, open a bottle of new Beaujolais, and convert the loneliness and despair to money and love.

I emerged from bottomland and cattail country and found the blacktop that led south into the Flint Hills. I listened to some Nat Cole, Julie London, and Rosemary Clooney. I didn't smoke. The air smelled of new hay and winter wheat. I even decided to teach Rita to spincast for bass.

I parked in the Scotch pines. Tiresias sat by the front door, his ears perked, his motionless body shiny and alert. Colby answered my knock.

"Mr. Roberts," he said. He wore some chinos, boots. He stepped aside.

Colby walked to the recessed stairs and spoke to Reynard. Then he disappeared into the back of the house, followed by Creon. Tiresias trotted through the door behind me. Reynard was on the zebra couch listening to a radio concert broadcast. Symphonic music stirred in the shadow patches of carpet. Stacks of paper and documents littered the glass coffee table. Reynard wore slacks and a white shirt.

"You've found something?" he said.

I walked down the stairs. Reynard lit one of his black cigars. Our game spread along one side of the table. Wind rattled the patio doors. Sun poured through.

Reynard said, "Colby and I were going over the books. I'm still trying to figure the skimming. I know revenue is constantly down, sometimes in small amounts, but steady. Our costs aren't up that much."

I sat on the zebra couch. Tiresias lurched down the stairs and heeled by Reynard's elbow. I lit a cigarette and riffled smoke into the silence. It was Mahler on the radio. I tossed the envelope onto the glass. Reynard heard it hit.

"What's this?" he asked.

"There's an envelope in front of you. Open it."

Reynard drew a fingernail along the seal. It opened, dropping the die to the glass. Reynard studied the die with his hands, rolling it in his palm, testing the contour with the fingertips. A curious expression crossed his face, amusement, consternation, comprehension, all at cross-purposes.

"I'll make a guess," he said. "Loaded dice."

"I took it from table one during my shift last night. Last night I cracked it with a knife. I dug one tungsten spot from the upper right corner of the 'one.' I scraped some paint from the other sides. There are half a dozen imprints. Tungsten, I suppose. The rolls are ones and sixes."

"Losers," Reynard said.

"Losers to you and me. If a guy gambled on the center of the table, making his bets on any craps and field, he would win money. I played with the die last night and when you miss a craps, you make a field bet easy. There's enough play in the dice to miss once in a while. That's just normal. If you didn't overdo it, the other players wouldn't notice for an hour. The dealer wouldn't take as long."

"You noticed?"

"I've been at the club for three days. In that time, someone has won consistently at table one. He plays for a couple of hours, then staggers home. He takes three or four hundred and packs it in. Streaks like that could cause revenue to drop. Don't you agree?"

Reynard rose. Tiresias rose. "Would you like a drink, Mr. Roberts?" Reynard extracted a leather leash from the side table and snapped it to the choke collar around the dog's neck. Together the blind man and his dog walked to the bar.

"Make mine orange juice or ginger ale," I said.

"You've taken the pledge?"

"Taking my work seriously. Drinking interferes."

Reynard mixed a Bushmills and water. He poured ice in a tumbler and covered the ice with orange juice. His movements displayed mystical dexterity in the sea of bottles and glass. He returned to the zebra couch.

"Who is the big winner?" Reynard asked. His voice formed ice, cold, violent, and spare. I felt he'd made up his mind to something.

"Look, Mr. Reynard," I said. "I suppose the winner might be accidental."

"That doesn't seem likely. Spill it."

"Three nights your son is the winner. He comes in around eleven, gambles for an hour, then leaves. He bets stupid, holds the dice for fifteen minutes, then hits a number and loses. He doesn't pay much attention and he's usually drunk."

Reynard struck glass with his fist. Spidery cracks erupted in the tabletop.

"I'll kill him," he said.

Reynard sipped some Bushmills. Mahler loosed a crescendo. Some of the chessman had toppled and I spent time rearranging the game. The shatter had brought Tiresias to his feet. He stood, eyes riveted on Reynard. Reynard shook the leash and Tiresias heeled.

"Is he working alone?" Reynard asked.

"I've paid attention to the action. I can't spot Johnny palming or cupping dice. He grabs the bones and rolls. When he walks to the table, I eye his movement and haven't spotted a dice switch. Besides, Mr. Reynard, I frankly don't think he's smart or sober enough to cheat."

"So he has inside help."

"What do you think?"

"My son isn't brave enough to cheat me alone."

"It would seem so," I said. Lucky smoke streamed into my poor lungs like flame.

"What kind of help would he need?"

"Gus Canard. Probably the dealer. I've talked to Tony enough to believe he's following orders. Probably doesn't have a stake in the outcome. It makes for good skimming."

"Make me another Bushmills, would you?" Reynard said.

I mixed the drink. Reynard unleashed Tiresias and snapped his fingers. The dog trotted through a side door and disappeared. Mahler drooped a notch, quiet, moody strings. My own musical taste ran to Louis Armstrong and Bach. I didn't understand lush, romantic stuff. I handed the drink to Reynard.

"How did you get the die?" he asked.

"I palmed it from the table."

"Do you think Tony noticed?"

"I doubt it. He glanced over as I picked it up, but I scooted in a substitute and it passed. I'll find out tonight, anyway. If they know, then the skimming will let up for a while. It will stop until I go away or until you are arrested."

Tiresias loped into the room, followed by Colby. Colby walked to the stairs and leaned on a rail.

"I'm here, Mr. Reynard," he said.

"Don't leave for town yet," Reynard said. "I want to talk to you for a minute. Roberts will be here for twenty minutes yet."

Colby said, "I'll be in back." He left.

Reynard shifted his attention. He sipped the Bushmills. "I want you to work a few more days," he said. "Keep your eyes open and report to me. Are you planning any more moves?"

"I'll look at the books tonight. I'll try to get photos. If

Canard is doctoring yours and keeping two sets, then you should be able to compare your books with the real ones he keeps for himself. If there's no difference, then your losses are strictly cheating from Johnny. In that case, I'd suspect Tony the dealer and your son are operating free-lance. It's been known to happen in casinos before.''

''I still don't think Johnny has the brains or the guts for it.''

Reynard placed his hands on the glass and explored the spidery cracks. He shifted some papers and pulled the chessboard to the center. He ran his fingers across the board, drawing the tips in an arc above the pieces. Outside, the sky revealed a frieze of clotted pink, sun and redbud and purple shade. A meadowlark tweeted.

''There's something else,'' I said.

Reynard hopped a knight. ''You've got trouble on the board,'' he said.

I studied the position, then moved a bishop. Reynard was right. I sipped orange juice. I'd been sober two days. My perceptions were aberrant.

''I followed Johnny after he left the club for the last two nights. He leaves at closing time. I shut down the table and I'm right behind him.''

''Why would you do that?''

I paused. The wind broke through the winter wheat in a fluid current. ''Agnes hangs on him when he plays.'' Silence crawled in the big room.

''Does he enjoy that?'' asked Reynard.

''I wouldn't know.''

''What do you know?''

''I know his car is parked at the house in Sleepy Hollow when I drive by. I don't stay all night, just two hours the first night. Agnes is there and Johnny is there and it's three o'clock in the morning. You make what you want out of it.''

Reynard stroked Tiresias. ''I told you I'd kill him.''

"Give it up," I said.

Reynard laughed. It was a sneer like a knife slicing skin, long and ragged. His hands and face turned white and his eyes tightened into a painful, wasted stare. "I've been on top too long," he said. "I don't give it up like that."

"It's time now."

"You don't know what the hell you're saying. Being small is your way. Being big is my way. I'll handle the trouble now that I know what it is."

"Your trouble won't stop just like that. No trouble does. You can't beat your way out and you can't buy your way out. Not ultimately."

"Get me the photos and we'll go from there."

"Then I'm through," I said. "My obligation to you ends at that point."

"Not until then."

"I made the deal, Mr. Reynard. I wish to hell I hadn't, but I did. I'll get the photos, then we're through. For myself, I've got a score to settle for Charlie Allison. That one is on the house. Then it's paid in full. I've been your eyes and I'll be through."

"You're washing your hands?"

"If you want to put it like that."

"Get the photos," Reynard said.

"You hurt Johnny and I'll come after you," I said.

Reynard paused. He puffed the cigar and sipped some Bushmills. The Mahler finished.

"You fucking punk," he growled.

"I wondered about you," I said after a while. "I felt sorry for you. But you bought me like you buy everybody else. Well, you've got your money's worth. But it's just about over. I won't look back. You do anything to Johnny and you're my business."

"Get the photos," Reynard said.

"If I can."

I stubbed my cigarette in a crystal ashtray and rose. Tiresias popped to attention and Reynard walked me to the stairs. Colby entered the room.

"Trouble, boss?" he said.

"No trouble," Reynard said.

I went outside into blue shadow. The pines whispered in a mild wind. Three brown squirrels cavorted in the pines, hopping and twirling acrobatically. I studied the perfect confirmation of a colt. He nibbled prairie grass and ambled to the brow of a hill, roan highlights glancing at sun. Through the window of the big house, I watched Colby and Reynard huddle. Reynard swung an arm violently. I drove down the gravel drive and away from Black Fox Ranch.

The highway was an empty, narrow finger. Suspicion clanked around my brain. It seemed likely to me that Canard had enlisted Johnny to run Jules out of the casino business, that the poison and horse killing and skimming were all a scheme to convince Jules that the gambling business wasn't healthy for him anymore. It seemed a rough way to deliver a message, but these guys weren't ballerinas and gambling wasn't dancing.

I wasn't close to discovering the killer of Charlie Allison, but the motive made sense. Whoever killed Charlie Allison probably wanted to frame Jules. That made it Gus Canard and Johnny. The only problem with that theory was the premise and the facts. Gus Canard didn't have time to close up and get to Maple Grove on the night of the murder. Perhaps he could have hired the job done, maybe one of the Syrian goons in the Canyon. I didn't think Johnny had the brains to kill Allison, but I'd been wrong on sure bets before.

Then there was Agnes. She gained if Jules took a fall. Maybe she wanted Johnny and the big house. Maybe Johnny would look better if he owned the Canyon and not just some crummy horse parlor in West Wichita. Maybe Johnny thought so, too, and planned this whole scam. Maybe

Truman shouldn't have dropped the A-bomb, maybe Plato was right and Aristotle wrong. Maybe I should learn to sew and get married. Maybe I could bake a cake.

The Canyon relaxed in a shaded cocoon. A gunmetal Cadillac was parked by the outside stairs. I parked and went inside.

Micki the hatcheck girl eyed me without interest. She clacked her gum and rubbed a stoic eyeball against her crossword. Black roots surfaced from a platinum swirl. I hiked past Taylor and headed for the kitchen.

Maye leaned in a back doorway, smoking a thin cheroot. She smiled as I approached.

"What's for dinner, Maye?"

"That all you think about? Food?"

"When you cook it," I said.

She laughed. "I could find you a steak, a small one."

"I'm through with it tonight, Maye. I thought you'd like to know. I haven't killed anyone and I haven't sold all of my soul. I think I can buy it back."

"I'm glad, Mr. Roberts," Maye said.

"We gardening together this summer?" I asked.

"Sure thing," she said. "You be here at seven for that fillet. I've got peach ice cream, too."

I winked at Maye and went through the swinging kitchen doors. Cowboys rode the bar. One couple nodded over spaghetti in a corner. The dance floor was lonesome as Quasimodo on Sunday afternoon. I strolled to table one and said hello to Tony. It was six o'clock.

I sticked for an enlisted man who felt hot. He dropped fifty dollars on field bets. The Air Force captain returned to the table and rode numbers, plowing the table steadily against rocky odds until he won a few dollars. He drank steadily and well. The enlisted man stayed away from the captain. He kept losing foolishly. The captain left the table.

I took my break and ate the fillet, garlic salad, and a

bowl of peach ice cream. By seven-thirty I was back on the table. The enlisted man had gone, replaced by a herd of Moose clubbers. The Moose club had slots, but no crap games. These guys were warming up for their meeting and some hot bingo.

Gus Canard sauntered through the casino twice, looking the place over like a raptor on a thermal. The blackjack tables filled. The casino developed a tense rush of energy. Two or three dolls in satin lined the roulette wheel, giggling as they lost their husbands' money, shouting when they won a small bet. There were more giggles than shouts, but they had fun. The mousy waitress brought me orange juice. I drank the juice and talked to Tony and sticked the table. The evening wore away like old shoes.

Johnny and Agnes arrived at midnight. As I watched them cross the busy dance floor, Agnes seemed flushed. They sat at the bar and ordered drinks and drank them. Agnes wore something diaphanous. Her bony legs were too bony, but she showed enough thin thigh to attract attention. Jukebox noise tore through the place like small-town gossip. Agnes dropped from her stool and led Johnny to the roulette table. They played and laughed like kids. The satin dolls left the wheel and discovered their husbands at the bar. The husbands looked like doctors.

Johnny Reynard strolled to a blackjack table and sat, slumped as a beaver coat. Agnes followed him on unsteady high heels. Some brown ribbon bound her auburn hair. The blackjack tables were sloppy and noisy with the drunken sound of people losing money and laughing over it. Soon enough, Johnny developed a small crowd. It surrounded him in an arc of humdrum motion. I couldn't tell if he was winning or losing, but money always draws a crowd. It's like a guy poised on a fifth-story ledge.

The gambling waned. Slowly, tables emptied of the sound of money and people. Johnny sat on his stool, hitting, staying, drinking whiskey. Agnes buzzed around him like a bad cross-examination. I watched the waiters stack chairs and busboys bus tables. The blond barman wiped the bar and stacked his glasses, then unloaded the cash register and rolled quarters. The cashier totaled figures. Tony and I wiped the crap table and quilted it. Tony stuffed some cash in a strongbox and stacked the chips. We hadn't spoken for two hours.

Gus Canard pushed through the glass beads and stood beside Johnny and Agnes. The fire-scarred black man swept the dance floor. He was a big man with roseate scars on his face, webbed fingers, and no thumb. Canard leaned against the blackjack table, taking up time and talking to Johnny. Agnes nodded and laughed. It was a thin, undistinguished laugh. Canard clapped Johnny on his back, then mounted the casino steps, shook hands with Taylor, and went outside. I walked to the bar and ordered a ginger ale for the road. The barman grimaced and poured the ginger ale. I downed some and left.

The night was cool silk and warm cotton. Summer stars burned through oak and hackberry shadow. Canard's Cadillac was gone and the windows of the office were dark. I felt for the camera under the front seat and put it in my pocket. Sweaty fear and determination gurgled in my stomach. I drove the Fairlane down the hill and went south on Hillside to a dead-end copse of mulberry. A clapboard shack hunkered down a dirt road. It was dark. I parked the car and walked up the crest of hill, then down the other side. From the brow of hill, I was directly above the Canyon, near Maye's hideout. I overlooked the stairs and the parking lot.

I opened the reel bag and examined the camera. I also had two jimmies, a small flash, pocketknife, and a screwdriver. Sweat drained into my shoes. Adrenaline whizzed in my brain. An owl hooted encouragement. Below, I could see a Syrian scrubbing dishes in the kitchen, his face bobbing in yellow steam. The burgundy Hudson and red MG were in the parking lot. Time froze.

I sucked air and moved. The office stairs rose before me. I stumbled up them, reached the top, and slid a jimmy into the lock. The lock wasn't complicated. Sweat and nervous energy shook my hands. That was complicated. The jimmy slipped and fell inside the tumbler. It clicked and the door opened.

Garlic and bad air rushed past. The office was dark as a coal shack. I pulled the door closed and stood sweating in black infinity. My eyes sought the details in the blackness. I flicked on the tiny flash and looked around.

I was beside the couch, awash in racing forms. I walked to the desk and rifled each drawer in turn. I unfolded the black ledgers on the bookshelves and found receipts for supplies, food, payroll records, and utilities payments. I found tax records, roast beef sandwiches, and a rubber. There was the detritus of a gambling history and nothing very neat. Canard wouldn't keep sloppy books for Jules Reynard.

The books were squirreled in a sideboard beneath a stack of racing forms and receipts. They were two hardback ledgers, blue ink, red lines, neat printing, dates, tables, and entries, all parallel and unequal. I studied the ledgers beneath a floor lamp, taking the chance that no one would see the glow. I spread the ledgers on the desk and snapped twenty photos. I folded the books and put them back in the sideboard. Then I snapped off the lamp and the flash and stood in darkness.

A scream spiraled in the night. My blood flowed north. Another low, terrified scream mounted and broke, followed by scuffles and a tangle of bleak, unsure cries. I stood in the dark as seconds flowed underground. I strained to hear and feel reality. I stuffed the camera and the jimmy into the reel bag. Thunder rumbled far away and then there was silence. I crossed the dark room and opened the outer door.

Wild night roared in the oaks. An empty parking lot spread before me, shimmering in the moonlight. I descended the stairs and stood in the dark, listening and watching. Movement spread in one corner of the lot like a stain. A figure huddled in the burst of lightning. Blood slammed in my heart. I moved for shadows and the movement itself.

As I moved in the darkness, I remembered Charlie Allison and the spidery crack of glass on Reynard's table. A black car loomed. My hands were drawn quickly into a V behind my back and I felt my head go down. There was the thick, sucking sound of bone and skin and metal together. I staggered in fields of pain, roaring bursts of it welling inside. I was part of the night and the metallic fear, bathed in nebulae, washed to a far shore of dreamless sleep. My head smashed into metal again.

I kissed earth. There was the struggle to breathe, a conversation, and a pair of shoes. I smelled Canoe and whiskey.

Then I was alone.

ELEVEN

"You've a concussion."

A cold shoehorn slid its way into my mouth. Gritty fog pounded my eyes above a glittering swath of broken glass. I felt hands lift my head and I drank water from a glass tube.

"There. You rest now."

I mumbled incomprehensibly from bandages.

"My name is Lucy, and Dr. Fiske says you'll be just fine. Rest, and you'll be up and around in no time."

Images sparred in a smoky ring, brown idols in raingear and mukluks. Mush dribbled in midair.

"Where am I?" I managed.

"Don't you worry. You're in the hospital, and I won't leave you tonight."

I groped after a face. I found an overfried bratwurst. I imagined myself sleeping in a leafy dell, water slipping from rocky ledges to deeply opalescent pools. A galaxy whirled into focus and became an isolated patch against inky darkness.

"What happened?" I said. My jaw throbbed. I raised my head. I lay in a white room, my tortured view directly on a white sink. Hollow white sheets hovered above me and something white spoke delirious sentences that made no sense. My tongue was a slab of gorgonzola.

"Help me sit up," I said.

"Don't be stubborn."

"I feel sick." I did, too.

"That's quite normal."

"More water."

Lucy was a nurse. She stuffed a pillow behind my head and allowed me water in small sips. The glass straw was cold and my head ached as the water fell into my throat.

"How long have I been here?"

"All day," the nurse said. She was nothing to me but a murky harbor full of rocking ships. Movement invaded my eye. Then there was strong shadow and solid form.

"How you doing, Mitch?" Another voice.

I recognized Andy Lanham. He was in a rumpled trench coat and drowsy felt hat. His face was an exhausted mask.

"Please don't try to talk," Lucy said.

"Turn on a light," I said.

"Don't be ridiculous," said the nurse.

"You look like shit," Andy said. "I told you to be careful."

Lucy felt my wrist. While she watched my pulse, I fought nausea to a draw. We each took our corner seats, waiting for the final bell. Cigar smoke corroded my view of the beautiful dames in the front row. They were there, I knew they were there.

"I'd like to talk for a while," Andy said. "I need to know what the hell happened."

"Will you be quiet," Lucy said.

"It's all right," I said.

"Don't be ridiculous," Lucy said.

Andy leaned above me. He was a pair of red eyes and a blob of mustard tie.

"What happened?" he asked.

"Will you two be silent?" Lucy said.

I thought it over. "Like I told you, I was making some photos of the ledger books at the Canyon. I got the pictures and came out of the office and went down the stairs. I heard someone scream, then a struggle. I walked into the parking lot and the next thing I know someone bangs me against a car.''

Lucy snorted and fluffed my pillows. ''This is ridiculous,'' she said. Then she sauntered across the room and read a *Life* magazine.

''You're a lucky boy,'' Andy said.

''I don't feel lucky.''

''Do you know who did it?''

''No idea. It was dark. Someone got me from behind, levered my arms into a V above my head, and slapped me against the hood. I don't remember a thing after that until your ugly mug.'' I sucked some tired water from a glass tube.

''You've got some deep bruises on your head.'' Andy sat on the bed. He took off his hat and wiped a hand across his face.

''I hate hospitals,'' I said.

''You're still a lucky boy. Any other impressions?''

''Well, there was someone else down there with me. A big pair of shoes. I can't be sure.''

''You say someone banged your head on a car hood?''

''That's it. Nice job, too.''

''Sounds familiar to me,'' Andy said. He took out a cigar and fiddled with it.

I wiggled my hands. They worked. I used them to hoist myself against the bedstead and look around. The nurse sat hunkered in a circle of fluorescence. Venetian blinded windows peered onto a redbrick wall, rising somber into a starry night. There were two chairs in one corner, and on a swivel tray at my arm there were utensils, thermometers, needles, and dials. The walls were white except for a putrid green stripe at shoulder height. Gray curtains hung wadded on a metal tube above me. The white toilet reminded me of my nausea.

I stretched and tried to concentrate. Pain knotted along my neck, arched in my back and shoulders. In place of my left jaw, there was a geegaw of wiry resistance. Hangovers and lost love were nothing compared to concussion. Andy dropped his felt hat onto my knee.

"Take it easy, boy. I do mean you are lucky," he said. "How do you feel?"

"I hurt bad. My head mostly."

"Doctor says you'll have to stand it for a while. They can't use painkiller on a concussion."

Andy licked his cigar and snuck a glance at the nurse. He needed a glass of beer and a smoke. Nothing but a long cruise with Rita on a small yacht sounded good to me.

Andy spoke. "Doctor says you shouldn't barrel race or do underwater photography for two weeks. No sex for ten years."

"That will make twenty altogether," I said.

Lucy dropped her magazine. She walked to the bed, took my pulse, and forced some water down my throat. She asked me how I felt and I told her. She mocked disgust and sat down with her magazine. I decided I would flirt in the morning.

"So, what the hell happened?" I asked Andy.

"You were meant to die," he said. He licked his cigar and looked at the nurse again. "I don't know why you're not dead, but you were meant to be. You should be with Charlie Allison right now. I don't know why you aren't."

"I don't understand."

"I don't, either," Andy said. There was conversation in the hallway outside. It drifted through a pine door.

"Why don't you tell me," I said.

"At three o'clock this morning the dispatcher at headquarters got a call from a woman. High-pitched, cracked voice, very excited. The woman said there were two seriously injured men under the Little River bridge. Asked for an ambulance and for the police. One of our guys got there a few minutes later and found you laid out on the bank. He could see that you'd taken a fall from the bridge, landed in the river like a bellyflop. Flat on your snoot in the mud. Broke your jaw and gave you a bad concussion. Ambulance brought you to the hospital and you've been here all day. Here we are."

Andy snapped his fingers and fiddled some more with the cigar. "You explain that shit to me," he said.

I struggled against the nausea. "Whoever pounded me against the car hood dropped me from the Little River bridge. They expected me to die."

"Ain't it a coincidence?"

"It sure is," I said. Sweat and fear drilled holes in my heart. Hot and cold shakes found my hands. "The same thing happened to Charlie Allison."

"You catch on quick," Andy said.

I tried to think. Nothing happened but pain. "You said there were two men under the bridge."

"Two," Andy said.

"Well, who was the other guy?"

"Johnny Reynard," Andy said.

Andy's words wormed inside and laid eggs. The eggs made glassine splotches in a bloody sack. There was a picture of me in the Ardennes forest, the dead-cold winter night like a dream around me, brutal, frozen, irrational. The dead men in my squad seethed with maggots, even in the cold. Then I saw worms everywhere, gnawing the bodies of Johnny Reynard and Charlie Allison.

"What about Johnny Reynard?" I asked.

"He's down the hall. He's in bad shape. Someone tore him to bits. His face is a pulp. Parts of it are gone—ears, nose. He's lost a lot of blood."

"Will he make it?"

"He was dumped into the river along with you. Whoever did it planned for both of you to die."

"But will he make it?"

"He will," Andy said slowly. "He's going to lose his sight."

A dreadful sickness overcame me. "He's blind," I muttered.

"His face and arms are shredded. Poor bastard."

Then Andy stood and wrapped the trench coat around his brown suit. He put on his hat and stuffed the dead cigar into the side of his mouth. Andy doubled and trebled in my vision. I raised my hands and examined the bandages on my head.

The nurse stood. "You should go," she said to Andy. She flipped off her reading lamp. A full moon drove blue shafts into the room, bars of it falling to the floor. The brick wall outside was like a block of ice. Andy and the nurse stood bound by striped moonlight.

"Who the hell made the call?" I asked.

Andy shook his head. "There's a hell of a thing," he said. "Both you and Johnny Reynard were laid on the riverbank like neat corpses. There was a towel under your head. Your damn clothes were wet and covered by mud, so we know you were in the river. Whoever called the cops took the time to wade into the river channel, drag both of you out, then put a towel under your head and look you over. Dragging you two through the mud and the driftwood was hard work, Mitch. Someone saved your ass."

"But why didn't they stick around?"

"I don't know. But you would have drowned." Andy walked to the pine door and turned. "Your pal Spud was here," he said. "So was Christine. Your mother and grandma are coming in this morning. I don't think they know the whole story, so make one up. I'll be down at the station house, but I'm going home now to get some sleep. I'll be by to see you later today."

"Who called the cops, Andy?" I asked. The nurse body-blocked the question.

Andy walked out through the pine door. Iodine and cold

steel slithered in. Lucy washed my face and gave me a pat. She cooed and I slept.

I woke buried in darkness. A shining moon bathed the brick wall. My feet were cold and my jaw throbbed. There was jungle noise in my head. There was also a shadowed mass submerged in yellow.

"Mr. Roberts?" a voice said. "Is that you?"

"Who is it?" I managed to whisper. Pain and powerless fear echoed inside my hollow skull.

"Are you all right? This here is Maye."

She moved into a puddle of moonlight. Her frail hands were clasped in front of a print dress. Thin shoulders huddled in a shawl. Behind her was movement.

"Maye," I said. "What are you doing here?"

Maye hovered above me like a sapphire.

"We saw the nurse leave and came in. We shouldn't be here now and we've got to go pretty quick. We don't want nobody to see us here."

Maye touched my face. She pushed aside some sweat and looked me over.

"My," she said. "You do look like something. I guess you're going to be all right, though."

"Maye, you can come to the hospital tomorrow. I'd like that."

"You don't know," she said.

"I don't understand."

"We done saw what they did to you," she said.

I waited. "Tell me," I said.

"You know how I go up on the hill and take a smoke and something to drink when my work is done? Last night I was up on that hill with some vodka and cigars. I saw what they done to Mr. Johnny Reynard and then I saw what they done to you. It was a terrible thing, but I saw what they done. It happened so fast, Mr. Roberts. I saw it when they took you away and I followed as fast as I could. I remembered you followed that other fellow, and that's what I done for you. I saw how they took you to that river bridge and how they bundled you out and threw you over the rail. I almost screamed out loud, Mr. Roberts, because I didn't think they was going to do that."

Tears welled in Maye's eyes and fell, sparkling, down the ebony edge of her cheek. She stood in fiery moonshine.

"How did you get me out of the river?"

Maye reached into the darkness. Slowly, some bulky shadows inched forward. From the black emerged the huge form of the fire-scarred man led into moonlight by Maye. He held himself slightly bowed inside work clothes. He twirled a cap in his big hands. Viscous scars knotted his face. There was no thumb on one hand. His oval face expressed gentle confusion.

"This here is Mr. Flowers," Maye said.

I choked.

"Mr. Flowers was on that hill with me. He went down the bank of the river and pulled you out and laid you on the sand. I called the police, and when we saw they came, we left. Mr. Flowers here done that."

The fire-scarred man stared at the floor. His cap made flannel circles.

"Maye," I said.

"Mr. Flowers and me, we're in the kitchen together."

"Maye," I said again.

"I know," she answered.

I looked at Mr. Flowers. "Thank you," I said quietly.

"He don't talk," Maye said.

I squeezed his big hand and it squeezed back. Mr. Flowers stared some more holes into the floor.

Maye spoke. "They put a dog on Johnny Reynard. It was an awful thing, Mr. Roberts."

Pale dawn anchored the brick wall. Opalescence rose like well water.

"You go home, Maye," I said. "I'll be fine now."

Maye and Mr. Flowers pushed open the pine door. My

room was silent then, filled by rose shafts. Pink tendrils ascended the brick wall. All around me in the morning, breath abandoned the dying.

TWELVE

Gray afternoon dangled in a bowl of daffodils. Grandma cried, Mother lamented; now, I was alone with pain and a gorilla in my head. A big nurse named Clara flowed into the room like Roumanian cement. She wore two or three chins tucked beneath a wad of Westphalian ham. One chin had warts. Translucent fat dripped from her arms. For twenty minutes she stuffed orange Jell-O and shaved carrots into my mouth, then followed them with buttermilk. The buttermilk hit like a sledge. Clara grinned and cooed, but the coo came out like a stertorous snore. She stuck my arm and drew blood, wrote on my chart, flipped on the radio. Then she raised two steam shovels and pounded out the door into the smelly hall.

I called Andy Lanham at headquarters and asked him to hurry to the hospital. He was interrogating a suspect and told me he would finish and come by. I asked Clara to check on the condition of Johnny Reynard and she told me he was in intensive care, blind and mauled. Clara said he wasn't talking and probably wouldn't for weeks. It made little difference. I knew what I was going to do and how.

I forced myself out of bed and paced the cold floor. I took fifteen minutes to cross the room, but I made it back in under five. I took off my cute nightshirt, found my clothes, and put on my white shirt. It was stiff with river water and caked as a week-old doughnut.

Furious dizziness struck and I sat down hard on the bed. Stars and nebulae and galaxies loop-de-looped in my funhouse brain. A pair of knives and forks tangoed along a puke-green beach. I lay down and the knives and forks stopped dancing. The dizziness passed and things started to make sense. I spent the afternoon thinking, dredging up logic and deduction. I knew who had mauled Johnny Reynard and who had used my head as a mallet. I knew who was skimming and I knew who was after Reynard and why. I had earned my fee, but it had cost Johnny Reynard his vision. There had been murder and enough brutality to put a Quaker off his feed for a month. It was time for the violence to end for good.

I phoned Jules Reynard. His voice cracked clear and cool across the miles.

"Where are you?" he asked.

"Never mind that," I said. "I'll be out to the ranch tonight at seven o'clock."

"There's nothing to discuss. You've told me what I need to know. My son is skimming and screwing my wife. I'll handle it."

"I'll make it hard on you if you're not at the ranch. I want Canard and Colby there, too."

"This better be good," Reynard said. Silence like atomic war descended over the miles. I heard Reynard breathe and then puff on his cigar. I imagined him reclining on the zebra couch, sibilant wind whispering from the lake, Tiresias and Creon erect like spikes.

"It will be fun," I said finally.

"If it's the ten thousand bonus you want, I'll have it delivered to your office."

"Keep the money. I've earned my fee. I want something else and it isn't money."

Reynard waited. Music joined the sibilant wind in my

mind. Separated by twenty miles of wheat and horse pasture, I saw Reynard clearly, vision rarefied by his own blindness, my own double sight by the acres of pain and money that divided our souls and views of life. Reynard calculated people as he calculated things, using them as means to an end, to humble, humiliate, and goad. He used people and used them up. Now I was used up and I was supposed to go away like garbage.

My own vision was nowhere as coherent as that. I hadn't the ability or the nerve to hover above people like a hawk, and I hadn't decided on any alternatives. My own hope lay in the land, taking nothing from the earth and staying quiet. People troubled me and I stayed away from them, becoming a hermit. It was killing me slowly, but I wouldn't be taking anyone with me. Reynard was taking everybody. I decided not to let it happen anymore. I'd give some of the money to Maye and Mr. Flowers, some to Spud, and then try to find ten acres along the Clark Fork River in Montana.

"Colby and Canard will be here," Reynard said. "After tonight we're finished."

"I'll be there," I said. I hung up.

Andy arrived twenty minutes later. He looked at the orange Jell-O scraps and stuffed a pudgy finger into the mess. He laughed.

"Next thing you'll be sucking milk toast," he said. Andy dragged an easy chair from the corner. He smelled the daffodils, looked at my chart, and took off his trench coat. He sat down and stared at me with big, liquid eyes.

"Did you get some sleep?"

"A whole six hours. Best for days. I still haven't touched my wife in a week," Andy said. "That's a hell of a note."

"It's going to be over tonight," I said.

"How'd your mom and grandma take it?"

"Lousy," I answered.

Andy said, "The D.A. is busting a gut. He can't play games anymore after what happened to you and Johnny. He has to make a real arrest or it's his ass with the voters and the governor. It looks like we've got a goddamn gang war, for Christ sake."

"I'm going to lay everybody out for you tonight," I said. "I want you to make the arrests."

Andy drew his face into a puzzle. There were deep, tired lines around his eyes and some fresh creases along his forehead. Age and strain were gaining on both of us.

"What the hell are you doing in that shirt?" he asked.

"You're taking me out of here."

"I am not."

"You are, too."

"I am not."

"We could do the Katzenjammer Kids all day, but I'm leaving this dump today."

"Suppose you tell me what this is all about. Maybe I'll play along."

"I'm going to Jules Reynard's ranch tonight at seven. I want you to come along about thirty minutes later."

"You can't do it, Mitch," Andy said. His voice lowered and he looked at me hard. "You're busted up bad and the doc says you need rest."

"And Charlie Allison is dead. He was twenty-five years old and never had a chance. Johnny Reynard is blind. At worst, he was a slob who didn't do any real harm."

"Tell me about it and I'll handle it," Andy said.

I got to my feet. The floor was cold as barroom love. Nausea cruised in a Cadillac with the top down.

"I can't do it that way," I said. "This is something I have to do myself before someone else gets killed."

"Who else could get killed?"

"Agnes Reynard," I answered.

Andy whistled. "The tootsie who married Jules," he mused. "Who would kill her?"

"Jules Reynard had a wife in Kansas City a long time ago. She crossed him and wound up bobbing for snails under a railroad trestle along the Missouri River."

Andy thought it over. He closed his eyes and relaxed into the chair. Frank Sinatra started to sing on the radio. He was pretty good.

I grinned. "Hell, you'll make captain out of this arrest."

"You're going no matter what I do?"

"Yes," I said. "Just like that."

Andy rose and buttoned my shirt for me. He pulled on my blue suit. It stank of turtle shit and catfish and had the strut and camaraderie of a life on its own. Clara came in the room and squawked like a two-hundred-pound rooster. She retrieved a doctor who lectured me on responsibility and health, my concussion, the Lord Jesus, and finally told me to go to bed and avoid aspirin. We left the hospital under a barrage of warnings, especially about booze. From the street, I heard Clara bellow.

We drove across town in Andy's blue police Plymouth. A gray sky frothed, purple-edged from the prairie north and west. Wind drew through the elms. On skid row the bums huddled in groups, sharing wine and silly talk; clots of bums parked outside pool halls, beaneries, and cheap cinemas. Women held down their skirts and men pinched their hats. Andy steered through the brick downtown and across the Douglas bridge. We drove above the river, murky with whitecaps and waves. We skirted right field of the ballpark and passed a row of boxcars. I heard the *plock* of fungos on horsehide and watched baseballs rise in arcs above the field, then disappear. Clouds thickened in the north and the wind steadied.

Andy rumbled through the alley and stopped beside the rabbit hutch.

"I had the Fairlane brought here," he said.

Mrs. Thompson hobbled down the stairs and stood holding Faith and Hope by the ears. Faith and Hope peeped and twitched their noses. Andy helped me into the house.

He sat me down on the bed and said, "I suppose I have to dress you."

"It would help," I answered.

Andy rummaged in the bathroom closet and found some pleated gray trousers, a red flannel shirt, wool socks, and Red Wing boots. He knocked around the oak dresser and extracted polka-dot shorts and a white T-shirt. We struggled for ten minutes with the ensemble. My head felt like a drive-in fight.

"How's your vision?" asked Andy.

"Double."

"Why do you want me at the ranch thirty minutes after you get there?"

"I want you to arrest Agnes Reynard for murder. Bring her with you. It will add considerable drama."

Andy sat in the gray overstuffed chair. I arranged myself on the bed. The sky turned yellow and the wind howled. Crows and starlings streamed north.

"Just what evidence do I have?"

"I'm telling you. Arrest her for murder and bring her to the ranch. While you're on your way, you might tell her about the gallows at Lansing. I want her to crack when we are out there."

"If this doesn't work, it's my ass with the D.A. And probably my badge. I can spare the ass, but I've got a wife and kids."

"Trust me," I said.

"With this trust shit and a dime I can get a Charles Atlas pamphlet."

Andy stared at my portrait of Carl Schlecter, a great chess artist dead of starvation in the second year of World

War I. Andy and I fought the second war and since then there'd been another. Experience bound us and I knew what he was thinking. He was thinking how complicated existence was and how impossible to understand, and finally, on a stormy spring night, that he was going to act solely from friendship and belief. It summed up our lives.

"Agnes lives in Sleepy Hollow?" asked Andy.

"Cater-cornered from the golf course."

"All right, goddamn it," he said. "I'll drag her out at seven-thirty."

"Take the highway east to Rose Hill Road and then south. Black Fox is a rambling ranch perched above a horseshoe lake. There's a red barn and some outbuildings. Gravel road into Scotch pines. Park there and come in. I'll unlock the front door. Just blast in like Buster Crabbe."

Andy threw me a windbreaker. "It's going to storm," he said. He walked to the kitchen and went onto the back porch whistling. From the back stairs he said, "I'll bring my ray gun."

I hobbled to the kitchen. A black sky boiled like mud coffee. I made some oatmeal and drank orange juice. I set the alarm for six o'clock and took a nap. When I woke, lightning creased the sky and there was sudden thunder. The heavens shimmered with ghostly orange light. My head was dull as a cinder block, but the double vision had cleared.

I washed my face and stared at the scarecrow in the mirror. He looked something like me except that he had bandages on his head and his eyes were ringed by blue-black bruises. He was a smiley helpful sort of guy, but he had a mean streak and no ambition. I brushed his teeth and told him to be polite and not drink so much. He followed me to the front porch and sat rocking.

I read Heidegger's *Being and Time*. Heidegger thought that being alive was like being "thrown" and constantly falling. It had the same physical unease and uncertainty as falling toward the unknown called death. We get used to the sensation and don't talk about it, but it's always there and always dark. The bottom is something that happens to other people, and when it happens, they are alone and nobody can help. *Splat*, you're dead and everybody says they're sorry and sends flowers and in two weeks you're a hole in the ground. Heidegger answered this with love, but he didn't think it was easy. I shut the book and hobbled down the back steps and got into the Fairlane.

Black storms north of the city advanced. The wind died to whispers, and along the creek bottoms small birds dug themselves into the grass. Streams of crows, starlings, and hawks sought refuge in cedar hedges and stands of scrub oak. The blacktop road struck south into electric distances, the sky everywhere a black cauldron of forces. The sun sliced through some clouds and broad rays of gold and mauve speared the earth. Then the wind died again, and there was the smell of ozone and hail. In the rearview mirror, I watched rain advance across the prairie like silver curtains above green wheat. Turgid yellow curled under the cloud and the rain smelled of iron. The temperature plunged suddenly, and there was an eerie silence.

I hauled the car into the gravel drive just as plops of rain struck the windshield. Canard's big Cadillac was parked in the pine lee. It gleamed like a weapon. Three quarter horses huddled against the red barn, tail to head. The Black Fox burned in the mist like a torch.

I walked to the front door and knocked for the last time. The door opened and Colby stood in front of me. His face was white and gray as sandpaper, the blue eyes sunken. He wore a white shirt and jeans, cowboy boots, and a dark leather vest. He looked smaller now, somehow violated.

He said nothing. I flicked the lock on the door and followed Colby into the room.

Two lamps burned brilliantly. Jules Reynard sat on the zebra couch captured by lamplight, our chess game in front of his face, the black and white pieces outlined by haloes. The big room was inert against the storm, the white carpet, the Klee, the philodendron, and the beige walls pressed by the black storm. Glass trembled in the wind.

Canard faced the storm, gazing at the boiling clouds. He had on the same black pants and rumpled white shirt. A bald spot on his head shone like grease, the hair a mess. He turned.

"Mitch Roberts," Canard said. "Some fucking guy."

"Shut up, Gus," Reynard said. Canard turned back to the storm. Colby walked to the stairs and stood silently. I went down the recessed stairs and sat on a couch facing Reynard.

Reynard ran his hands above the white pieces and moved a piece. I checked him and he moved his king. He smiled when I moved and took a rook.

"You're in for it," he growled. Reynard shoved a bishop across the board and sat gloating. The end was near and I knew it. He played brilliantly.

"You're not very damn good," Reynard said.

I lit a Lucky. "I told you to leave Johnny alone."

"What is this shit?"

Reynard couldn't see my bandages and black eyes. Our chess game was over and we were playing with real lives. The rules were the same, but the stakes were higher.

"The game is over," I said. "It's not over the way you think. I told you not to move on Johnny until I had a chance to check the books. I told you there was a chance he wasn't skimming and I wanted to make sure. You couldn't wait. You had to make a move and prove you weren't helpless."

"Keep talking," Reynard said. "I love to hear shit dribble."

"You had it all figured out. So you put a dog on Johnny because you believed he was skimming and sleeping with your wife. I told you the evidence wasn't in and I wanted you to wait for me to learn the truth. You thought you knew the truth. Maybe you wanted to believe Johnny did it. You're more than blind, Reynard."

"You're talking junk," Reynard said. "You can't prove I did shit to Johnny and neither can anyone else."

"I can prove everything."

Canard walked into shadow and stood looking at me over a crystal lamp. "Hey, Julie," Canard said. "I don't know anything about Johnny skimming, I swear. I didn't do Allison."

Reynard lit a cigar. His face was pure Kabuki, shrill and mysterious.

"It's something I'll take up with the boys in Kansas City," Reynard said to Canard. "You know what happens to guys who cheat me."

Canard wiped sour sweat from his face. He stank of garlic and kibbe.

"Johnny is blind," I said. "Torn to shreds."

Reynard's face sought Colby. "I heard he was dead," Reynard said. Colby moved against the stairs. Thunder crashed to earth. "I said, I heard he was dead," Reynard said.

Colby said, "I guess not." Reynard raised his head to me.

"He'll be blind a long time. But he's alive," I said.

Thunder pealed again. Lightning snaked like fingers across a black, boiling sky. Rain increased in gusts.

"It's your move," Reynard said.

"Pay attention," I said. "My first night at the Canyon I watched Colby, Canard, and Bunch beat up Charlie Allison, throw his body in the backseat of Bunch's Buick, and drive him away. I told you that, but I didn't tell you I followed the Buick into Maple Grove. Bunch and his goon tied Allison to a slab with a note on his lapel and then they drove away. I looked at Allison and he was alive. I know he was working for the reform candidate and this game has been played before. You run the guy out of the casino and everybody goes about their business. But something happened this time.

"You see, what I didn't tell you was that I was in the cemetery when someone in a big car pulled in and drove right to Allison. That someone shot at me. I didn't know who it was, but it had to be someone who knew where Charlie Allison would be. I worried about it, but the next day Charlie Allison was dead. I could have stopped it, but I thought it was going to be all right."

Canard walked to the stairs and stood beside Colby. I watched them but didn't see a gun. Tiresias and Creon trotted into the big room. Reynard sensed the dogs and snapped his fingers. Each reacted and took up positions beside Reynard like sentries. They flinched when thunder struck.

I continued. "My suspect for the Allison killer was someone connected with you, obviously. That made it Bunch, Colby, or Canard, or one of their goons. After the poison and the horses, it was obvious someone was trying to run you out of the business at the Canyon. Colby and Bunch and Canard may have had a motive to bump you. You own the clubs and take the profits. Maybe those guys were tired of stooging for you, so they figured to force you out. It looked open and shut.

"Bunch didn't do it. I knew that right away because he had his chance and instead he tied Allison down and drove away. I didn't think Canard had time to leave the club and follow, but he could have had a goon follow. Colby could have done it, but I didn't figure he stood in line to inherit the Canyon. Maybe he was working for Canard."

Colby shouted, "Don't listen to this punk."

"Be quiet," Reynard said. He puffed the cigar. I waited for the thunder to cease. "It's still your move," he said.

"Like I said, I couldn't figure Colby for the Allison murder because he had no interest in the club. If something happened to you, the club belonged to Canard and Bunch. In fact, with you out of the way, Colby would have nothing. That seemed to let him out."

The storm progressed. Tense silence grew like a spider web, a strange, magnetic calm.

"Then Johnny came on the scene. He had motives, all right. I watched him cheat the Canyon three nights running. I watched him drive to your wife's house and stay. It seemed to put him on the hot seat.

"But last night something strange happened. I snuck into Canard's office and found a set of books. They were duplicates, except for the figures. Canard was skimming on paper, taking the profit and leaving you with a set of fake books. It proved Johnny wasn't skimming by table cheating. If there had been table cheating, then Canard wouldn't have needed two sets of books. When I left Canard's office, I wasn't sure what Johnny was doing, but I knew he wasn't skimming. I couldn't decide where the crooked dice came from because I didn't think Johnny had the guts to cheat. He'd never won before, and that seemed to confirm that he wasn't a cheat. But the crooked dice came from somewhere. I took some pictures of the ledgers, but I don't have the film because I took an unscheduled bath. But the skimmer wasn't Johnny."

Reynard controlled his disbelief. He ran his hand along a dog's flank. Hair bristled on its spine. Low growls erupted like magma.

"I don't believe it," Reynard said. "Gus."

Canard was silent. He lit a cigar, and we all listened to the wind rage. Waves on the lake rolled. "The guy is full of shit," Canard said. "He can't prove it."

"What's my motive for lying?" I said to Reynard.

"All right," he said. "Go on."

"A few days ago I started thinking. Someone killed two of your horses. You may remember my first day here when I hopped the rail. I had to hustle back because those yearlings were wild as hell. It started me thinking. Then I talked to a veterinarian in Augusta named Glick. He told me the dead horses were unbroke yearlings. He said the horses were torn up and Colby was burning the carcasses when he arrived. You assumed the horses had their throats cut and I took it for granted you knew. It sounded right at the time. But, Mr. Reynard, they didn't have their throats cut."

"What are you saying?" Reynard asked. Now the wind tore through the prairie, howling. Rain stretched and drove in fists.

"Those horses were on six hundred acres. Nobody could have gotten close to those yearlings. Certainly not two of them. Even if you had experienced cowboys down here, it would have taken two or three jeeps and a lot of time. I don't think it happened that way."

Reynard bowed his head. "Dogs," he said.

"Dogs," I said quietly

"Let me do this guy," Colby said. Reynard stroked the dogs.

"I don't get any of this," Canard said. He wiped his face.

Three sets of headlights broke the storm and weaved up the gravel drive. Chunks of time broke away like icebergs. The big door opened and Andy stood in the doorway, wind and water flowing around him. He held Agnes Reynard by her arm and her eyes were wide and alarmed.

"What the hell," Reynard said. Canard and Colby stared at Andy. Colby moved.

"Take it easy, boys," Andy said. He dragged Agnes

into the room. The door banged in the wind. "Some of my police pals are outside." Andy smiled.

Agnes wore Andy's trench coat. She looked like a wet cat, small and scared. Her auburn hair struggled on her head like cake batter. Rain swept into the room.

"Who is it?" asked Reynard. His voice rattled in the storm.

"My name is Lanham. I'm a lieutenant in Homicide. Mr. Reynard, I've just arrested your wife on a murder charge. She's taking it for Charlie Allison." Agnes sobbed then, big welts of fear in her chest.

Agnes looked at Colby. "Tell them," she begged.

"Shut up, you whore," Colby said. He edged for the bar. Andy watched him. Canard hung on to the stairs, surprise and fear on his face. Lightning illuminated the prairie.

"Let's everybody relax," Andy said. He stared at Colby with malice.

"Back to last night," I said. "I'm in the parking lot and someone knocks me out. But first someone puts the dogs on Johnny. Then someone dumps both of us in the river and leaves us for dead. Only there were two witnesses in the parking lot who saw everything. They can identify the people who tried to kill us."

"Who are these witnesses?" asked Reynard.

"Forget it," I said. "I'm here and Johnny is alive. You asked Colby to put the dogs on Johnny. I know he can handle them. Since I showed up in the parking lot, Colby decided to kill me, too. He probably realized I had seen the double ledgers and could clear Johnny."

"I'm not saying anything," Reynard said.

"All right," I said. "But you know Colby can handle the dogs. You have to figure he killed the horses, too." I paused to smoke. "Why do you suppose Colby would poison you and kill the horses? Why do you suppose he would kill Allison, if he did, and hope the blame comes to you?"

"You tell me," Reynard said. "Like you said, he won't get my business."

"He wanted your house, your oil, and your money. He wanted your wife, or maybe he was just using Agnes as a way to get everything you owned. It was Colby."

Agnes slumped and wailed. Sobs racked her and rain swept into the room. Thunder crashed. Andy put his hand into his suit pocket.

"Colby set up Johnny," I said. "Johnny wasn't cheating the Canyon and he wasn't skimming. He didn't know shit about skimming. The guy skimming was Canard. He made a duplicate set of books and took you for a percentage. Johnny was set up, and I figure Colby knew Canard was skimming and took advantage of the situation to blame Johnny."

Canard waddled back to the crystal lamp. "Look, Julie," he said. "You been around a long time. I wanted my fair cut, that's all. But I didn't do nothing else and I didn't do Allison."

"He's telling the truth," I said. "Canard was cutting you down with the books, nothing else. He didn't kill Allison and he didn't set up Johnny."

"Tell them." Agnes sobbed. "I didn't kill anybody," she said.

"Shut the hell up, will you?" Colby said.

I went on. "You hired me and Colby started to worry. He saw an opportunity to kill Allison and he knew you'd be blamed. He didn't scare you away by killing the horses, so he thought he'd pin a murder on you. Colby doubled back to the cemetery and killed Allison by throwing him into the river. He wanted the D.A. to come down on you. With you out of the way, he could have Agnes and your money."

Andy watched Colby. Agnes slumped like old luggage. She was finished crying and her eyes were vacuums. Colby leaned on the bar and stared into the storm.

"Like you said," Reynard replied. "He can't get the club. So what's his motive?"

"Agnes," I said.

Reynard lowered his face. The blood was gone from him.

"Colby is the man," he said.

"Yes," I said. "You blinded your son for nothing."

Agnes broke away from Andy and stood pleading with Reynard. Rain and tears streamed down her face. Her voice became shrill and hysterical.

"I didn't kill Allison," she screamed. "I tell you I didn't. I helped Cole because he said we could have it all. But I didn't kill anybody."

Colby sprang on Agnes. He struck her with his fist and she went down like a sack of magnets. She screamed. Colby kicked her with his boot. Andy drew a revolver and trained it on Colby. For a time, the scene was static.

Finally I started talking again. "I don't know how they got Johnny over to Sleepy Hollow those nights. I do know Agnes substituted dice so I'd believe that Johnny was table skimming by cheating. They wanted me to report to you that Johnny was cheating and sleeping with Agnes. That's what happened, Mr. Reynard. Colby and Agnes knew if you found out that Johnny was doing that to you, you'd have him killed. They knew you. Then the cops were supposed to arrest you and then they'd have your house, your money, and your oil. They didn't give a damn about the Canyon."

Agnes raised herself. She sobbed. "I had benzedrine. Johnny came over for that. He was crazy for benzedrine. Colby found some and Johnny would pass out from benzedrine and liquor. We knew Roberts would see his car."

Colby kicked Agnes again and I heard his boot drive in with a dull, sick thud. Andy crouched and moved, driving Colby back with the revolver

"This scene is over, folks. You're under arrest, Colby," Andy said.

Reynard struck the dogs and they rose instantly. Snarling, they sprang on Colby. He screamed and staggered back to the bar. The dogs tore into him as he screamed. There was a sickening sound of teeth and a furious fight, wild with broken glass and tangled furniture. Blood and broken flesh appeared as the dogs found Colby's neck. I whirled as Andy fired his first shot.

"No," screamed Reynard.

I dragged Agnes aside and watched the dogs tear Colby. Andy maneuvered above the man and dog. Two uniformed cops ran into the room. Andy fired twice and the dogs fell.

"Get the sheriff and an ambulance," Andy said. One cop ran back into the storm. The room was quiet except for Agnes and the rain.

Andy and I knelt above Colby. Reynard stayed still, his head buried. Black blood pumped from a gash in Colby's neck. Two pale eyes stared ahead, unseeing. His face was burned hamburger.

"I don't know," I said to Andy.

"Wrap him up," he said.

I found some towels behind the bar, then wrapped them around his neck and pressed. The uniformed cop returned with a first-aid kit and began to work.

The second cop came in. "They're on their way," he said.

"It might not be soon enough for Colby," Andy said.

"I don't know," I answered.

Colby twitched, but the black blood pumped into the towel.

The uniformed cop took over for me. Andy and I rose together and walked past Agnes to the front door. Reynard's face was blank. Canard huddled on the stairs. Andy and I stood outside in the night. I lit a cigarette and Andy sucked on a cigar. The wind died and a pale moon rode the clouds.

Then across the black, wind-tossed prairie we heard a siren.

JULES REYNARD–MITCH ROBERTS, played at Black Fox Ranch near Wichita, Kansas, during the first week in May 1956.

KING'S GAMBIT

	White (Reynard)	**Black** (Roberts)
1.	P-K4	P-K4
2.	P-KB4	PxP
3.	B-B4	Q-R5 check
4.	K-B1	P-QN4
5.	BxNP	N-KB3
6.	N-KB3	Q-R3
7.	P-Q3	N-R4
8.	N-R4	Q-N4
9.	N-B5	P-QB3
10.	P-KN4	N-B3
11.	R-N1	PxB
12.	P-KR4	Q-N3
13.	P-R5	Q-N4
14.	Q-B3	N-N1
15.	BxP	Q-B3
16.	N-B3	B-B4
17.	N-Q5	QxP
18.	B-Q6	QxR check
19.	K-K2	BxR
20.	P-K5	N-QR3
21.	NxP check	K-Q1
22.	Q-B6 check	NxQ
23.	B-K7 checkmate	

ABOUT THE AUTHOR

GAYLORD DOLD was born and grew up in Kansas, where he has settled after living in San Francisco, London, and Fort Lauderdale. In addition to writing the Mitch Roberts mystery series, which began with HOT SUMMER, COLD MURDER, he is a practicing criminal attorney in Wichita, Kansas. In his vanishing spare time Dold collects books, trout fishes, and follows boxing and Double AA minor league baseball.